MW01382910

The Breed

JAMES W. OWENS JR.

ISBN: 1478381256
ISBN-13: 978-1478381259

DEDICATION

This Book is dedicated to God first and foremost. God gave me a dream one night and instilled a passion in me to make it into a story. Also to my Lord and Savior, Jesus Christ, it was His sacrifice we have the ability to receive salvation. The power of His name gives us authority over the presence of evil and the kingdom of darkness.

John 1:1-5 NKJV

In the beginning was the Word, and the Word was with God, and the Word was God. He was in the beginning with God. All things were made through Him, and without Him nothing was made that was made. In Him was life, and the life was the light of men. And the light shines in the darkness, and the darkness did not comprehend it.

CONTENTS

ACKNOWLEDGMENTS

Juanita Owens, your un-wavering support, helped me finish this book. You have inspired me in so many ways. You stuck by me and never stopped believing in me. Thank you for being there for me, even when I doubted myself.

Jered Campbell, who is like a brother to me. Thank you for the time and effort in designing the graphics and artwork. It was beyond my expectations.

John Boddington, if it were not for my wife getting a haircut, we may never have known about your editorial talent. Thank you for all your hard work and dedication.

PROLOGUE

Chris was 17 years old when he began

researching and wanting to learn about the dark

side of spirituality. He was so intrigued by

what he was learning that he decided to keep it

from family and friends. He had a much deeper

passion and a different outlook on his life than

his family. Chris was searching for power

rather than purpose and could no longer see

himself as the Christian he was pretending to

be. He was traveling on a path one should not

want to go down, but Chris was determined and

this determination would change his life and

those around him forever. Sometimes things

are not always as they seem, always what we want, or even what we seek.

Chris was born into a God fearing Bible believing family that went to church every Sunday and Wednesday. His parents, Conner and Theresa, are devout Christians and serve at their church in different rolls. Both of his parents came to know Christ as teenagers through their youth group this is where they began dating and eventually got married. Raising their children in church was their mission. Their goal was to see their entire family come to salvation. They had four children two boys and two girls; Marcy is the oldest, then Chris, Sammy and Stephen. Life was great and all was on track or so they thought.

CURIOSITY

"Christopher," his mom calls.

"Yes, Mother," he answers in disgust because he does not like to be called by his whole name.

"I need you to come downstairs, and join us for breakfast."

"I will be down soon. I am just finishing

up some last minute homework."

"Fine, but hurry so your food does not get cold."

"OK, Mom, I got it."

Chris is searching on his computer for a spiritual store where he can buy research books rather than just looking on the Internet. This way, he can read the books, and hide them, or he can read them when he is not at home.

"Ah, good morning, Chris," his father says in a happy voice.

"Good morning, Dad, hello, everybody." Chris states sarcastically.

"Well, gosh, what a greeting," says his sister, Marcy "aren't we just grumpy today."

"Enough!" Mom yells, "Let us pray."

Taking in her next breath she continues,

"Father, thank you for the blessing you have bestowed upon our family, thank you for the love and care you give us mercifully everyday, bless this food, which you have provided, and bless our home. In Jesus' name we pray, Amen."

"Why do we have to pray over our food?" Chris said sarcastically.

"Because God has blessed us with all that we have and without Him we would not be blessed." said Marcy as if Chris did not know.

"But I just don't see the point to all of it, Marcy. Why do we always have to pray, always go to church? Doesn't God know what we want and what we will do anyway?"

"Yes, Chris, God does know." Connor butts in, "but it is not about His knowing, it is about our obedience to follow Him, and acknowledge His word and what we are suppose to do to please Him."

"I just don't get it. Why can't He just accept what I do and who I am?"

Connor thinks for a second.

"Well, Son, it does not work the way we think it should, but how God thinks. He is not upset with you, Chris. He just does not accept our sin or a sinful lifestyle. He wants us to repent and turn away from our sin, not to continue in the same sin after salvation."

Chris cannot help himself from starting to argue.

"So then what you are saying is, I have to do what He says without regard to how I want to live?"

Connor starts to get frustrated.

"No, Chris, that's not what I am saying, you need to listen and not block your mind, you need to hear the truth not what your mind is telling you but your heart."

Chris cannot stand this conversation anymore and rudely exclaims,

"Whatever, I am done. I have to get to school!"

Connor senses there is something wrong with Chris and turns to his wife.

"Theresa, we need to pray for Chris."

"I know, Connor, we need to ask for his salvation. He is young and confused, we need guidance from God on how to handle this."

Theresa turns her attention to Sammy for a split second. "Sammy, can you please hurry up,

I need to take you to daycare."

"Connor, will you please get Stephen to school, I will take Sammy to daycare, but you will need to pick her up after you're done with work?"

Connor is half listening as he tries to finish the rest of his breakfast. "Yes, Dear, I will take care of it, and can you bring dinner home with you tonight?"

"Yes, that's fine, I love you, have a blessed day."

The family returns home from their long day at work and school. Chris spends most of his time upstairs in his room reading a book he has purchased from the Internet about Satanism.

The rest of the family spends their time

discussing the possibility of going on vacation. Connor suggests maybe going to Israel so the family could visit the Holy Land. Theresa was not so sure about the idea because it was a big expense. She was thinking about something simpler like Yosemite or even Yellowstone National Park. She tells Connor that they could rent an RV, but he was not interested, so as usual, the discussion was over with no results.

Chris walks downstairs with his book and decides to sit in the study to compare the book with the Bible. Chris caught Theresa's eye, so she decides to approach him.

"What are you doing, Chris?"

"I am doing research on different religions."

"What kind of religions?"

Chris, feeling interrogated, replies with an attitude.

"Well, Mom, your religion and the one I'm interested in, Satanism."

Theresa's skin crawls as she tries to talk some sense into Chris.

"You know Satanism is of the devil, it is his deception and darkness?"

Chris is now annoyed at his mother's constant remarks about how he should seek God. He decides to let his feelings be known.

"I don't care, Mom, I am judging for myself. I have a right to see what is best for me, and maybe your God and mine are two different people, two different entities, and one makes sense to me and helps me understand my life without condemnation. I want to be free, and your faith or religion does not make me feel that way. Your God expects a lot, whereas my god only expects what I can actually do or care about doing."

Theresa's heart starts racing as she suddenly realizes what she is up against.

"Chris, I am sorry you feel this way, and I wish I could say something to help. I don't want this evil influence coming between our family. You need to respect our home. We do not want this demonic force here."

Chris is now starting to see he must make some choices if he is going to continue on this path.

"Fine, Mom, whatever, I will find people like me and do what I need to do."

Chris stomps out of the den and goes into

his room.

"Honey," Connor calls.

"Yes," Theresa responds as she looks at the clock.

"I need to get some things done for work, and I am on a tight deadline. Can you do some online research for me?"

Time has slipped away and it is getting late, but Theresa agrees to help.

"OK, Honey, I will get to it shortly."

Suddenly, Theresa realizes Sammy is not in bed yet.

"Marcy, can you please tuck Sammy in for me. I have to help your father?"

Marcy is always willing to help with her younger sister.

"Yes, Mother, no problem."

Marcy comes out of her room and yells to Sammy.

"Come on, Sammy, get into bed."

Sammy is playing with her toys and does not want Marcy to put her to bed. "No, I want Mommy!"

"Well Mommy is busy, Sammy. She told me to tuck you in. I am sure Momma will still come kiss you goodnight."

"Ok, Marcy, but can you read me my little lamb story, please?"

"Yes, Sammy, I will."

While Theresa is doing Connor's research online, she notices some disturbing sites that were recently visited. She immediately knows it was Chris and yells,

"Connor, I need you to come here please."

Annoyed at the interruption, Conner replies,

"What, Theresa, I told you I'm busy, and I have a deadline."

Sensing Connor is a little bit annoyed Theresa remains calm.

"I know, Babe, but please, I have to show you something."

Connor stops what he is doing and begins to get up.

"OK, I am on my way."

When Connor enters the room Theresa explains,

"See, Connor, this is what troubles me. Chris has visited an online site that deals with satanic rituals and sacrifices."

A little taken aback Connor responds,

"Oh, wow, that's not good. I knew Chris was curious, but I did not know he was this in-depth. It looks as though he actually wants to engage in these things. He apparently has sent out requests for people who are in the area and interested in learning about a dark religion. We need to pray and then talk with him about this. It could get out of hand very quickly."

Connor and Theresa pray together and then call for Chris.

"Chris," Connor calls without a response so he calls again this time with emphasis, "hello, Christopher!"

"What…what do you guys want now?"

"Hey, we just want to talk, there's no need to start up with an attitude, OK!"

"Well, I don't have one, but fine, I am on my way down."

Chris closes his book and once he reaches the bottom of the steps he blurts out, "OK, what do you guys want?"

"Well, your mother saw some sites that you apparently went to and we wanted to ask you some questions?"

Chris shrugs his shoulder with a no care attitude.

"Well, what do you want to know?"

"Well, to be honest, we want to know why you are looking into Satanism."

Chris finally has his chance to come clean. He does not like hiding anymore and wants his family to know where he stands. "Well, Dad, it's no big deal. I'm just looking to see what it is all about. It is not like I am going to kill someone or something. I am just comparing Christianity with other stuff, and yes, Satanism is one of them."

Trying to make sense of the situation Connor inquires, "Well, Chris, it is a dark road to go down. Why haven't you researched things like Islam or Buddhism, why just Satanism?"

"Oh, my god, really. I cannot do all of them at the same time and this one caught my attention. It has built up a level of curiosity that you will not understand. You will never understand me, you will never see what I see, and you will never have the passion and satisfaction that this could bring to me. I will be free to be me without condemnation from you and your Christian ways. I am me, and I don't need your God. I will explore what I want and choose what I want, just leave me alone. I can decide for myself!"

Chris runs upstairs and slams his door, and begins to cry, for he is not sure of anything but the curiosity that is within him.

ENGAGING

Six months have passed since Chris and his parents talked about the information on the computer. Theresa and Connor have prayed very hard and have not given up on him. Chris has turned 18 years old and has decided to no longer associate with his family's church. Not too long ago, Chris met a man named Zaga who is a member of a satanic church. They have been meeting three times a week for 1-3 hours each time. It has been Zaga's influence on Chris that has captivated Chris's mind, and has turned him from the Christian Church completely. Zaga is a deeply spiritual man, and he believes the powers of darkness make rejecters of Christ stronger than Christians. Zaga's philosophy is to gain control by showing the powers of darkness and the acceptance without judgment of others. Chris had asked to be a member of the dark spiritual entities. Since then he has tried to show his friends the freedom he possesses. Chris seems happy, but because he was raised in church, he is still battling inside himself.

The effect on the family has been shaky. Chris's parents and siblings sense the evil and the force that has taken control of him so freely. His parents weep for him daily, and even though it may seem as if nothing is changing, their prayers have not been in vain. Chris is almost totally withdrawn from his family and is fully engaged in the satanic lifestyle. Chris wears a necklace with the pentagram and a ring on his right hand with the numbers 666. He has told his parents he is a child of the world and that he feels powerful and free. His parents told him it wasn't real freedom. The power may be real but he is now an adversary of God. God will not see him as an enemy but the devil is now inside their son. Marcy is in a tailspin of emotions. Her family seems to be in a state of turmoil since Chris has gone astray. She has asked her mom and dad for advice on what to

do. She is devoted to God and loves her
brother, but she does not want to see the enemy
destroy her family. Her parents simply tell her
all she can do is pray, and Chris. To let the
light of Christ shine through her, in hopes of
piercing the darkness that has fallen over him.
Sammy, who is too young to really understand
what is happening and so vulnerable to the
mayhem that could soon be unfolding, is in the
watchful eye of her sister Marcy and her
parents.

"What will happen when Stephen comes
home from camp?" Marcy asks as she
approaches her mother.

"Stephen is a strong young man. He will
devote his time to prayer and seek God as we all

are," her mother replies.

Stephen, who is now 13 years old, has spent two weeks at summer camp with the church youth group. He does not know the extent to which his brother's behavior has changed. Chris is slipping faster and faster into the arms of Satan. Stephen would be an easy target for Chris to try and recruit into his newfound faith.

Marcy, who is now 20 years old, has decided to look into going to college. She has devoted most of her time to mission work, but is still not sure what she should do. It seems the enemy has begun to wage war on her family.

Confronted by his family about his new venture into Satanism, Chris insists and tries to convince them it is not about worship. It is only about power and acceptance and he feels accepted by his new peers. His parents feel differently because his appearance and attitude have changed. He has been slandering Christians daily. He even burned a Bible at a meeting with Zaga and his new friends. He has totally renounced Christ openly, to all who know him.

Chris's appearance has changed. He is wearing all black and he looks very gothic. He only listens to hardcore metal feeding on it day and night. Christian music has no place in his heart or life anymore. Chris is now closed off to his family, and his family is in constant prayer for him. Life must go on, so everyone is coping the best they can. Parents are working, Sammy is learning and growing, Stephen is concerned for his brother, but continues his normal activities, and Marcy is still deciding about college. Life is moving along and chaos is not strong, but the presence of evil is becoming more and more prominent. Since Chris started engaging in darkness, Conner and Theresa have been engaging the enemy with prayer. They can sense a brutal spiritual battle on the horizon.

Connor puts in a requested for his Pastor to come and pray over the house. He feels a strong, satanic influence invading the family. Pastor Shane was more than happy to answer the request and set up an appointment to come by, in a few days. Theresa and Connor have decided to move Sammy into their room and move Stephen into Sammy's old room. This would bring the kids closer to them. They do not want Stephen close to Chris since they do not know what kind of influence Chris would have on him.

It is apparent that the family is becoming a little fearful of the life Chris is living, especially since he has publicly renounced Christ and has stated he hates Christians. They do not know where they stand in his heart at this point in time, but in their heart he is their son, and they will never stop loving him and praying for him.

Marcy and Chris have not spoken to each other in about two months, partially because Chris wants nothing to do with her since she is a born again child of God. Does he still love his family? This question cannot yet be answered, as he has a lot of hatred, and has distanced himself away.

"Should we ask him to move out, Connor?" Theresa blurts out as she thinks about protecting the family.

"I don't think that is the right thing to do at this time, Theresa. Chris needs to see God in us, and we need to know what is going on with him as much as we possibly can. He is quiet right now and not bothering us except with his lack of respect and bad attitude. We will have to stay on top of what he is doing and see if he advances in the darkness. Time will tell all, and we have to be ready for whatever is going to happen with him."

As the weeks go by, Chris engages deeper

and deeper into the satanic fields. He is now seeking the possibility of becoming a warlock or a satanic priest. He has surprised many members of the group he joined, because he is demonstrating some unforeseen powers and it makes him feel like a special person. These powers come from the devil himself, but why? What could Satan want to use Chris for? Could he have given him certain powers to attract others? All that is certain is Chris is advancing in power so much that even Zaga is beginning to submit to him. Zaga now feels like he is the student instead of Chris' teacher.

Zaga taught Chris much of what he knew about reaching the dark world of spiritualism. Zaga has never seen a person so focused and so intensely motivated to learn and seek as if his very life depended on it. It seems to Zaga that Chris is finding things more and more interesting the deeper he digs into darkness. Chris has spoken with demons that he calls, *the glorified spirits of darkness*. He asks for things that no man should ask for and soaks in the evil that dwells around him. His engagement with the spirit world has captured his heart, mind, body and spirit. He invites them to use their powers through him making him powerful and respected. He is fully engaged and ready, he has rapidly progressed and, is, shall we say, now the leader of the group that took him in.

Chris is moving out of his parent's home in a few weeks, and his parents are questioning this move.

"I must leave for we cannot co-exist together, you and me. If I do not leave, there will be nothing left of you. My lord says I must abandon you and go so you will not be a hindrance to my calling, and no war shall be called. Do not attempt to stop me or get in my way. Do not call upon your God for me as I am in the care of the god who has chosen me. He is the rightful god, and he shall reign in great glory. I will help him attain his rightful place and be a prince in his kingdom. I am sealed with his presence and have powers to bring others to myself for a great life and journey that they will love as I now love."

As Chris leaves to go upstairs, Pastor Shane comes to the house. Connor answers the door and tells the pastor what has just taken place. Pastor Shane comments.

"We are going to be careful with this. The enemy is tough against a man who is weak-spirited and has a lack-of-faith. We need to seek God and ask Him what to do. For now we will pray over the house, but expect some interference while Chris is here. The enemy has entered your gates, Connor, and we must now engage him with the right plan of action. Engage to remove his stronghold from your home and your family, for safety in the wings of the almighty God. A battle is coming and we need to be ready. This is not a battle against Chris, but a battle against the forces of darkness in which Chris is the target. Both sides want him, but he has chosen his side blindly, and we have to fight for his freedom. It will be a freedom he will have to see and want. This is not something that we can force upon him. God gives us a free will to choose whether it be good or evil. We will need to keep praying and be strong for Chris. The powers of darkness are no joke and certainly not a game, but we have the almighty God on our side and when the time comes there will be a tough fight, but we will be the victors."

"Thank you so much for coming over, Pastor, we appreciate you. We will do what you have suggested and we will become stronger. We will battle for our son."

As pastor Shane leaves, Connor and Theresa sit down in the living room to soak in all that is happening to their family.

"Well, Connor, I think the pastor is right,

but when will we know the time is right for us to do battle?"

"Theresa, we are in a battle right now, praying for him is a battle, but we have not reached the point where pastor Shane said we will be going. I am not sure what we have to look forward to, but I do know that we need to be ready.

God, our Father show us, guide us and lead us into your righteousness to fight the battles that will soon come to pass."

EXPULSION

A month has passed since Pastor Shane went to visit the family. During his visit, he prayed with them and over the house to get rid of the evil presence. The new school year has started and Sammy is now in kindergarten. Stephen has begun eighth grade, and Marcy has decided to go to college in her hometown so she can live with the family. She decided to major in religious studies and minor in psychology. Her semester is full and she will be quite busy.

All has been pretty peaceful in the home since Chris moved out. Life has been sad, and the family is doing all they can do to keep busy. They continue to pray for Chris, it seems to lift the heavy burden, because they have not been able to speak to him since he left. He has not wanted any communication from his family he has, in a sense, expelled them from his life… or has he?

Connor and Theresa have relied heavily on their friends, family and fellow church members. This has been a hard journey and having the comfort and support of everyone has helped alleviate some of the pain for them. Sammy is not as affected by what has happened. She is so young and innocent and only interested in having fun like a normal 5 year old. Stephen, on the other hand, is having a more difficult time. He escapes his feeling of abandonment by going to youth group. He loves here. going on youth retreats and special events, it reminds him of the times he would spend with Chris. Now he spends his time alone listening to his favorite bands feeling lonely and forgotten. Chris was more than his big brother. He was his buddy and best friend. Stephen would like to lean more on his father, but he is always busy with work and does not get to spend much time with him. His sister, Marcy, spends as much time as she can with him, but college has her busy. When they do get a chance to be together, they love to watch movies and go ice skating. Unity seems to be crumbling, because everyone is doing their own thing independently.

Sammy keeps asking her mom to take her to the park so Theresa made some time to take her. As they arrive at the park, Theresa sees a member of her church named Kelly.

"Hello, Kelly."

"Hi, Theresa, how are you doing? How's the family?"

"Things have been so hard for us. I just wish things did not have to be this way. Chris has not spoken to us since he moved out. Stephen is going through a lot because he feels so alone with Chris gone and Connor working a lot. I just don't know how much more we can take, Kelly."

"Well, Theresa, we have you all in our prayers, and if you and Connor need someone to help with Stephen and Sammy, just ask. You and your husband need to have a break and spend time together as well. Remember, you have a church family who loves you all, including Chris. We are all praying for God to move in your lives. We love you and are here to help in any way we can."

Theresa is so grateful for all that Kelly said to her, she is overcome with emotion, and tears ran down her face as she put Sammy in the car.

"Why are you sad, Mommy?"

"I am not sad, Sammy. I am full of joy and peace and thankful for the friends God has placed in our lives."

"Does that mean God will bring my brother

home to us, Mommy?"

"That is all of our prayers, Sammy, we hope for that someday."

As Theresa and Sammy arrive home, Connor's car was sitting in the driveway. This was unusual because it was only three in the afternoon. Connor does not usually get home until later.

"Connor," yelled Theresa. "Hello, Connor, where are you?"

"I am in the study, Honey, what do you need?"

"Why are you home so early, Honey is everything OK?"

"Yes, Theresa, everything is fine, I took the afternoon off to spend time with you guys, I have had no time with anyone, and I have lost one son already. I will not lose another one."

"Connor, Chris is not your fault. You did a great job as a father. You loved him and taught him things. You did not fail. God did not fail. Chris chose a path that he believes would make him who he wants to be. He is just blind, Connor."

"Theresa, please, I know what the issues are I don't need you telling me time and time again. I can't deal with it. I am hurt and angry. I don't know what else to do, my son won't talk to me, to his family, we mean nothing to him. I am heart broken, and I have reached my limit. I am broken, Theresa, I am broken and I don't want to lose another son or daughter.

God, please help me. Help us Lord, we are crying out to you. We are shedding tears of hurt Father. Comfort us please. Heal our broken hearts, God. Please don't let me lose another child, Lord."

After 20 minutes of crying and praying together, Connor walks up to Stephen and wraps his arms around him.

"Son, I love you so much. I am sorry for not making time to be with you."

"It is okay, Dad, I am not mad. I know we are both hurt that Chris moved out."

Stephen hugs his father tight. "You are my hero, Dad. Someday I want to be just like you. You make me so proud, because you care for us and provide things we need. You are a great dad and I love you and mom so much."

"Well, Stephen how about we get us a set of tickets for that concert coming to town in a few weeks? We can make a day of it together."

"That would be so awesome, Dad, yes, let's do it!"

Marcy comes home just before dinner, and the family brings her up to speed on the day's events. Marcy understands everything her family is going through, but she is not ready to open up and share her feelings. She has not told anyone how sad she feels inside and how Chris' absence is affecting her. She desperately wants to tell Chris how she feels, but he will not have anything to do with her.

Marcy locks herself in her room as she looks at pictures of Chris. Every night she prays for him as tears run down her face. He used to love her so much that he would have given his life for her. She asks God to help heal her broken heart. Marcy tries to understand why he is doing this and why he does not care about them anymore. Eventually she falls asleep with a heavy heart.

It seems Chris's goal of achieving power has worked without him even realizing it. The enemy has used him to destroy the joy that was once so strong in their lives. Maybe he can't see it anymore, but deep down inside he knows what it has done to him and his family. He does not care. His hatred for his family and Christians is growing stronger each day. He no longer fears anything.

At 10 a.m. on Saturday morning, Pastor

Shane drops by to visit the Smith family and see how they are holding up.

"Hello, and good morning, Pastor."

"Hello, to you as well, Conner. I wanted to come by and visit with you and your family, see how things are going and how you're holding up."

"Well, Pastor, we will admit it has been harder than we thought. We have had emotional breaking points, and we just cry out to God and ask for him to heal our broken hearts."

"Well, I can understand, Connor, I have felt in my spirit there is heartache, sorrow and a heavy burden over your family. Connor, let me tell you that none of this is your fault. You did not do anything to cause this and could not have prevented it. This is the free will of one person, one young man who decided in his heart what he was going to do. Remember, he may not be thinking with a clear mind, but his ways are true to him and his life now has meaning as he sees it. Again, all we can do is pray for him, and of course, we need to pray for your family during this trying time. Focus on God, Connor, seek his face, and be the pillar that your family needs you to be. I know it is not easy, but you must be strong and stand your ground or the enemy will finish you. Not in the sense of your lives, but rather your family life as you know it. Do not give him any more ground than he has taken already. Prepare for battle, Connor, we had this talk before, and you must prepare yourself for the fight."

After Pastor Shane left, Connor felt a little better and worse at the same time. He is trying to understand what he needs to do to be prepared for the fight. He does not know what to think because he does not know who it would be against. Would it be against Satan, or a battle against his very own flesh and blood, Chris? Will he be able to do what is necessary or will he battle uncertainty and fear.

Whoever this is going to be against, Connor has a lot of praying and preparing to do, because whether he knows it or not a battle with Satan has already begun and has taken over Chris. Not because of anything Connor or Theresa did, but rather the free will of their son. They cannot see the big battle coming, but God can and as long as Connor and Theresa seek him, He shall be their refuge and strength and lead the charge against the powers of darkness. Christ is the Lord of their home and the presence of the Holy Spirit will rise up and defend against evil.

As the weeks went by, the family has been doing a lot of Bible reading, soul searching, and praying. Leaning more and more on God and seeking him every day they have grown closer and closer and Marcy has been doing better with her grief. Connor is being more of a leader in his family by taking the time to be a husband and a father who not only provides financial support, but also spiritual support and helps his children understand God and His ways. Everyone has been very receptive and has grown on individual levels. Yes, they are going in a great direction, and they have even been more involved in their church. Stephen has taken up playing guitar for his youth group band, Marcy is involved in the singles ministry now and helps feed the homeless on Friday nights. Connor is helping in a ministry called, *Lost but not Forgotten*, in the church, which helps parents cope with children who have strayed away from God and their families.

Theresa is leading a women's group to encourage the nurturing of children with stories of the Bible at a child's level. She has been very successful in leading new mothers at the church with the reading of scripture that will captivate their child's attention. She devotes this time on Saturday morning to enable her to be free in the afternoon so she can take Sammy to the park. They have been having a great time bonding at the park together and sometimes Marcy meets up with them to be a more attentive big sister to Sammy. Things are looking up for the Smith family, and even though they know rough roads are ahead, they are enjoying their time together while preparing for the future.

THE CALLING

Since moving out, Chris is staying with a group of people who have the same views as him. The house is large and has many rooms. The hallways are dark and lit only by candles. The floors creek when you walk on them and an evil presence can be felt. Each member of the group has their own room and the extra rooms are used for common places and offices. When Chris joined the group, Zaga became his mentor, a person he could look up to, learn from, and grow. In the past few weeks, Chris grew so much that Zaga is no longer a person Chris needs. Chris is leaning on a supernatural power that goes beyond his comprehension.

Chris has recruited several people into the group. The group is now looking to Chris as a leader instead of Zaga. Although Zaga is not jealous, he has had words with Chris about what is taking place.

"Chris, come here I need to talk to you."

"Yes, Zaga."

"You are developing in a rapid way, and I am worried you are taking things too far. You are being looked at as a god, Chris. You are no god, only a man."

"Well, Zaga, I understand what you are saying, but why are you acting so jealous of me? Zaga, don't get me wrong…"

"SHHHHHHH, Chris, please just stop right now, you need to listen to me. I am still the head and leader of this group."

"Zaga, I don't care what you claim to be."

"Shut up, Boy, you need to listen to me, we have had this talk before."

"You shut up, Zaga, you have no power over me, and you need to watch your step."

"What are you trying to say, Chris?"

"I am saying that you can claim to be the group's leader but I am my own, you are nothing over me. My lord is Satan, I have chosen to except him and heed to his leadership."

"Chris, what the heck are you doing, this is not about worshipping evil things. We just want a free spirit to enjoy life."

"Zaga, you know what we are about, or I would not be here. Do not argue with me! DO NOT TRY ME AGAIN!" Chris' voice changes into a demonic tone.

"What the? UH, OK, Chris, or whoever you are, OK let's just settle down here."

Chris looks Zaga in the eye and walks away. Chris knows he has to find out what people are on his side, so he tries to find Jessie.

"Jessie, are you here?"

"Yes, Chris, I am here."

"I need to talk to you."

"What do you need, Chris?"

"You are one person I feel like I can trust right now. Since you have joined us, I feel connected to you. You are a smart girl, and I need someone I can trust with things I need to share."

"Well, of course, Chris, you can trust me, I look up to you so much. You are a great spiritual man and an influence to us all who seek to be with the darkness. I am your friend and servant. I will obey whatever you command."

"Wow, Jessie, that is great, but I am taken aback. I didn't know you felt that way towards me at all."

"We all do, Chris, I cannot believe you could not tell."

"Well, I thought everyone looked up to

Zaga, and only saw me as a recruiter to give them guidance into a new world."

"Chris, with all due respect, your powers and your spirit are more than that of Zaga. He fears you. He is not sure what he needs to do, but he will not surrender to you."

"Why not? He should be able to see what I am becoming."

"What are you becoming, Chris?"

"I am growing in power. I feel strong inside and I feel the darkness within me. I will be the one who makes all the decisions and plans out our goals and missions. Are you with me, Jessie?"

"Yes, Chris, of course I am devoted to you, and the one who gives you power.

"Find out who else is with us and get me

their names. I will make a point very soon. For now, I am going to speak with Zaga."

Chris walks back to Zaga's office and knocks on the door.

"Zaga, hello, it's Chris, I need to talk to you."

"What do you want, Chris?"

"Can I come in and sit with you as we talk?"

"Yes, that is fine, come in."

"Well, Zaga, I want to apologize for losing it with you earlier, I should not do that to the person who took me in and had me under his wing."

"Well, Chris, I appreciate that, I feel as though you are acting selfishly with things. You still need to mature and learn things. What you do or whom you choose to call god is your decision. I personally do believe in Satan, but I do not worship him or call him my god. Why do you feel you have chosen to do so?"

"You know why, Zaga, I have spirits inside me that have shown me the true god and his powers. I am now at their disposal."

"That is a dangerous road, Chris. I heard the demon speak from you when you were mad at me. The demon uses you to fulfill what he wants. I know about possession, my mentor was possessed but I never could invite them in. I am afraid about what they would do with me. I am not willing to go that far with things, Chris."

"Well, Zaga, I am, and I am there already, I hate Christians and those who oppose my god and me. This group needs a leader who has the power to stand and to fight. Are you prepared to do that or not?"

"Are you giving me an ultimatum, Chris?"

"In a way yes, I want to know you will lead this group in the right direction, Zaga."

"Chris, the direction of this group was and always has been to aid those who need refuge, to seek what they want in fulfilling their spiritual needs. That's what I have done for a lot of people including you. So if you are asking me to step down my answer is NO! I will not surrender my group or the people I have helped!"

"Zaga, understand what I am saying, if you are not with the vision that has been given to me, then I am not asking you, I am telling you that you will no longer be in charge. Out of respect for mentoring me and others you will be kept on, but that will be all."

"Who do you think you are coming here and telling me you are demoting me, and tell me what I will be?

"I am my masters' son. I have been called to start a revolution, an uprising against all who stand against my god. That includes you, if you get in my way. Who am I, you ask, who are you, Zaga? You have no power over me!"

As Chris storms out of the room, he decides to go see Jessie in the main parlor area. When Chris arrives, he sees a large number of people, approximately 20. He is happy to see such a large group.

"Jessie, hey, did you get the list we spoke

about?"

"Yes, Chris, and it was overwhelmingly in your favor. I feel weird though because Zaga took us in and helped us all with our struggles."

"Yeah, well, things have changed, and he needs to know we are growing and evolving in our spirituality. I am tired of feeling held back by him. I have gone further and I am in contact with our lord and his angels. The dark prince is my leader now, not Zaga. He needs to join us. How many people do you have on the list, Jessie?"

"Well, all but two: Zaga and Tanner. I never approached Zaga and Tanner is afraid of what Zaga will do if she goes against him."

"Well, I will talk to her and make sure she understands Zaga cannot do anything to her for joining us. The time will come when everything will be lined up and in order. There are things coming, Jessie, and I want to start preparing us for those things."

Chris walks down the hallway to Tanner's room.

"Tanner, hey, it is Chris."

"Oh, hey, Chris, what's up?"

"I wanted to talk to you about what is going on."

"What do you mean?"

"Well, I know you are a little jittery about things because you are afraid of what Zaga may think or do."

"Well, no, Chris, I am not afraid of that."

"Then, why did you say you would not join us to stand against our enemies?"

"I do not think we should make Zaga feel like we don't care about him, that's all."

"I don't want him to feel like that either. I had a talk with him, Tanner. He does not want what we want. He is afraid of change and the powers I am obtaining."

"Well, I think for now you need to drop it, Chris. I need to figure things out for myself. I don't need you deciding for me, OK?"

"Fine, Tanner, whatever. I am going to go anyway, I have things I need to do. I will talk to you later."

Chris leaves Tanner room and decides to go see Jessie. She has a way of lifting his spirits and making him happy. As he walks down the hall to Jessie's room, he thinks about what he is going to tell her.

"Well, Jessie, I think things will become interesting over the next few weeks. I have tickets to a concert if you would like to go with me."

"Of course, I am flattered you would ask me."

"Well, I feel a real connection with you, Jessie, and I would like for us to know each other more. I know it seems odd but I am for real. You have a wonderful spirit and I am so happy when I am around you. You feel what I feel and see what I see and you support me."

"Well, yeah, I mean I totally feel the same way, I just never said anything because I was, well lets just say, I wasn't sure you would be interested in me."

"Well, Jessie, I am, and maybe this will

become something serious. I am excited, this concert is supposed to be really great."

"Who is the band?"

"They are called, *The Lost Sons*, and I have heard them, they are fantastic. So, it's a date then?"

"Oh, for sure, I can't wait to go."

"Cool, I will talk to you later then, OK, Jessie, I have some other things to do right now."

Chris spends time alone in his room. He meditates about the plans he wants to see come together. He is very quiet and secretive, although he confronted Zaga, he is still undeterred in his plans. No one knows what those plans are or when they will happen.

Chris finishes his quiet time and decides to go out and see about some supplies he needs. While he is out he has a close encounter with Pastor Shane. He walks in the store to shop and he sees Pastor Shane so he heads in another direction.

Pastor Shane sees Chris.

"Hello, Chris."

Chris hears his name, but totally ignores him by turning around and walking. Pastor Shane stood there a little shocked and then walked away.

As Chris is checking out, he looks out the window at the same time Pastor Shane looks back, before getting into his car. The two lock eyes, and Chris gives an evil look and says in his mind, *"the next time he sees me he will regret that he even knew me or tried to befriend me. This God lover will see my true presence when the time is right, until then, he knows by my stare that he should never try to trade words with me. In time, he will see and he will know that I am not afraid. His kind presence will not trick me and he will not want to challenge me if he knows what's good for him."*

GROWTH

Connor and his family have been enjoying the spiritual and personal growth with God and each other. Stephen is playing in the youth group band, Theresa is doing great with her group, and Marcy is doing great in school.

The family overall has a great new dynamic, which is making them stronger. Sammy is such a blessing to the family. She is an innocent spirit and she makes the family laugh.

After church, on Sunday morning, Pastor Shane asks to speak with Connor, so they walk to Pastor Shane's office, in the back of the church.

"Connor, I wanted to let you know that I saw Chris in the store last night."

"You did, Pastor?"

"Yes."

"Well, what happened? Did he say anything to you?"

"No, Connor, he was distant and quiet. He didn't respond to my greeting at all. As a matter of fact, he gave me a very daring and evil look as I was leaving the parking lot. To be honest, Connor, I am really worried about him."

"Thank you for sharing that information with me, Pastor, I will let Theresa know about it."

"Well, Connor, that's not all I have to say."

"Oh, what else is there?"

"I felt an enormous presence of evil around him. It seems to me that Chris has gone farther into his desires and by that I mean I believe he is demon possessed. This makes him extremely dangerous to himself and others, because he will have to obey what they tell him. It is sad to say, but I feel like that is exactly what he wanted."

"Oh my, Pastor."

"It's ok, Connor; I know it is hard to hear

but I needed to warn you about it."

"Well thank you, Pastor, I am just in shock, I guess. I didn't think Chris was going to fall prey to that. I really felt like it was just a phase and he would get over it and come back home. But now it is obvious that this is real. Again thank you, Pastor, I will pray and seek God about this."

"OK, Connor, have a blessed week, and if you need anything feel free to call me, OK?"

"Sure will, Pastor, and please keep us all in your prayers."

Conner leaves the office and walks back to the front of the church where Theresa is waiting for him.

"What was that all about, Connor?"

"Well, Pastor Shane told me he had a little

run-in with Chris, at the store last night."

"He did, oh my goodness, how did it go?"

"Well, he said he tried to reach out to him, but Chris just ignored him."

"Really? I didn't think Chris would do that. I thought he would have at least said "Hello" back or something."

"Well, Theresa, he said the only thing Chris did was give him an evil look as Pastor Shane left the parking lot."

"WHAT! WOW! I cannot believe that he would do that to Pastor Shane."

"Well, Theresa, he did, and Pastor Shane said he sensed an evil spirit from Chris that he has never seen before."

"WHOA! If he felt that then does that mean, like, oh no, no please tell me it isn't…"

"Yes, Theresa, he feels that Chris has invited demons to possess him to give him strength and power."

"OH NO, PLEASE NO, NOT MY BOY, JESUS, PLEASE."

"Theresa, it's OK, Honey, we need to pray for him and battle for his life."

"But, Connor!" Theresa cries, "I can't fathom the thought, of the enemy living in my son, I can't right now I just can't."

"Theresa, we are in this together. I am hurt too, but we need to be strong and allow God to shine his light through us. Connor starts to pray.

Father God, pierce the darkness within Chris please, Lord Jesus, please do what you can do to reach him. Don't let the enemy destroy him with lies, deceit and the ideas of greatness in that kingdom."

As the Family returned home, they noticed that there was a note on the front door. Connor walked up and took the note.

"It does not say who it is from, Theresa."

"Well, open it anyway."

"OK, here we go… Dear Smith family, I am writing to you to inform you that you may be in danger. I know your son Chris and I obtained your address from his personal address book. Please forgive me for this invasion. Chris has become very obsessed with his love of Satanism. I fear that as he grows stronger and more powerful that you may be in great danger. He has taken over our group from Zaga. I am only in the group out of fear that if I

do not stay and look to him for all my needs
that he will kill me. I will remain anonymous,
but please be warned. Guard your home and
your family, he can no longer be trusted, he is
turning into something supernatural.
Something I have never seen before. I have
been a follower for years, and I will tell you that
you either stand with him or you are against
him. I am not sure all he is capable of, but I do
know that he has stricken many with great fear.
Again, I am sorry for invading your privacy,
please destroy this letter, as I do not want it ever
getting back to him, thank you."

"Wow, how interesting was that, Theresa?"

"Um, I am speechless, but I do wish we
would have known who this person is. I wish
that we knew because this person seems to have

a soft heart and not an evil one. This person can be reached, Connor."

"Yes, Theresa, but unfortunately we don't know who this person is."

As they made their way into the house, Sammy is whining because she is tired. Theresa takes her upstairs and puts her down for a nap. She walks back downstairs and sits on the couch. Theresa is startled at the sound of the phone ringing. It is Pastor Mark asking her to get Stephen from band practice, because he is not feeling well.

"Hey, Marcy."

"Yes, Mom?"

"Hey, can you come down here please?"

"OK, Mom. What's up?"

"Can you go and pick up Stephen from band practice, please. He wasn't supposed to be done for another hour, but he told Pastor Mark he wasn't feeling well, so we were asked to pick him up. I have a lot I need to get done right now, so I need you to go."

"Sure, Mom, I don't mind."

"Thank you, Marcy, I appreciate it so much."

"Really, Mom, it is no big deal, I've got it taken care of."

Marcy is now on her way to get her little brother from band practice, as she arrives at the church, Stephen was waiting outside the youth room.

"Hey, Stephen, I am here. How are you feeling?"

"I am not feeling well, Sis, I feel dizzy and like I am going to throw up."

"Oh boy, that's not good, well let's go, OK? I will get you home to Mom, and she can check you out."

On the way home, Marcy and Stephen were talking about the band and how things are going. Stephen told her that he was doing really well, and that Pastor Mark was teaching him a lot.

"Wow, Stephen, that is really great! I am so proud of you."

"Thank you, Sis, I just wished that Chris were here to see how good I am getting."

"Well, Little Brother, it is his loss, but I understand how you feel. I miss him too. Just remember to keep him in your prayers, OK?"

"OK, Sis, I will."

Marcy and Stephen make it home.

"Hello, Mom, we are home."

"Oh thank goodness, how are you son?"

"I feel dizzy, and sick to my stomach."

"Well go lay down, and try to rest.   I will call the doctor to see when I can get you in, OK, Honey?"

"OK, Mom, but please don't call me *honey,* it is so girlie."

The Smith family tries to have Bible study and prayer every chance they get. Conner decides tonight would be a good night to gather together and study.

"Hey, everyone, come on down."

"On our way, Dear."

As Theresa approached the study, Conner notices she is alone.

"Where is Stephen?"

"He is not feeling well so it will just be you, me and Marcy. I put Sammy to bed already."

"Oh, OK, we will pray for him after Bible study"

"What are we going to study, Dad?"

"We are going to study John, Chapter 1 tonight. I will go over the first five verses and we can discuss how it speaks to each one of us. OK, so John, chapter 1, verses one though five says this "*In the beginning was the Word, and the Word was with God, and the Word was God. He was in the beginning with God. All things were made through Him, and without*

Him nothing was made that was made. In Him was life, and the life was the light of men. And the light shines in the darkness, and the darkness did not comprehend it".

"What does this say to you, Marcy?"

"It tells me that Jesus was in the beginning with God the Father and the Holy Ghost. They have been since the beginning, but the focus is on Jesus, He is the Word, the light of the world and when He came to earth the darkness of this world could not understand him."

"That is a very good explanation, Marcy, I don't think we can say it any better than that; however, it has another meaning to me. As a father, it tells me to let God's light shine from us to reach the lost, to reach those in darkness like Chris is in right now. I feel that even though the darkness cannot understand the light of Christ, we can still penetrate the darkness with him and reach them for His glory. I feel very passionately about this and I feel it is a calling in my life to fight the powers of darkness."

"Wow, Dad that is very powerful."

"I say it, Marcy, because I am going to fight the spiritual fight for my son's life, for his eternal life, and for his life here on earth and I will not rest until God's will is done. So Theresa, what did the scripture say to you?"

"Well, to be truthful, I feel as if it is God telling us that we need to put Him first. Jesus is and will always be first, He is the word of God and the light of the world. Not all will receive Him and that includes Chris. Maybe Chris will never accept Jesus as his savior, but I can have hope in Christ and pray for my son to receive God's gift. I love God, I praise Him and thank Him for his son. His son is His word and when we hold our Bibles, we are holding Jesus, the very heart of God. I see God calling us to be in His service, but not to change people. We cannot change anyone, it is Jesus who changes people and He will come to those who call upon His name and seek His face."

"Theresa, that is so great, very powerful, God is truly speaking to our hearts, and I know He will reveal what His calling is for us to do. Not only with our son Chris, but also for other people we will encounter. We will be His tools to work His will and spread His word. Marcy had great points, we all do, I think we will be moving forward and maybe we should have more than one bible study each week."

"Yes, definitely, Dad, we need to do this."

"Great, let us pray.

Father God, thank you for the blessings you have given to our family. Thank you for your son Jesus and the gift of eternal life. We pray to you and ask in Jesus name that you will reach Chris, call him to you. Be with all of our children and protect them Father. We are blessed to have such wonderful kids and no matter what they fall into Lord they are still our children. They are your children Father, we all belong to you, use us and teach us to fulfill your will God. We ask these things in Jesus name, AMEN."

THE BREED IS BORN

Chris has become increasingly close to Jessie since he found out she was attracted to him. Chris invited Jessie to a concert that is coming to town, and she accepted. As the day draws near, Jessie and Chris have been talking to others in the group about how he wants things to be. Daren, who is another member, expressed his concerns about the group. Chris always listens to the members express their point of view.

The group is comprised of twenty members. The main members of the group are: Jessie, Tanner, Daren, and Thomas. Thomas has come from a childhood of drugs and poverty. His mother was a drug dealer and was killed over a bad deal when he was 12 years old. After his mom was killed, Thomas went to live with his grandmother, she was a Godly woman, but Thomas was not into church, much like Chris. The main difference between the two is Thomas has no siblings, or parents, and his connection with Zaga is very strong.

Daren is from a very wealthy family, and

his family is not religious. In fact, Daren has been involved in Satanism for quite a long time and was an influential part in grooming Chris into it. Zaga does not consider himself a Satanist. He considers himself a spiritual father to the hurt and lost that find him. Zaga, who is 45 years old, does not want to fight or cause division in his group. He is a peaceful man who cares about the people he helps. He has helped many people gain confidence and finish high school. A father figure and a friend, who does not judge or tell his group how to live, but rather to treat each other honestly. It is now apparent to him that maybe his control or leadership is hanging in the balance.

Chris calls a meeting with Daren, Thomas,

Jessie and Zaga. This meeting is about leadership, goals, and the organization of spiritual needs. Chris asked Zaga to begin the meeting at 7 p.m.

"OK, people, we are here to talk about things and make resolutions for the benefit of this group. The big topic here is Leadership. Chris mentioned to me that he feels he is ready to lead this group and take care of you. What I would like is to hear what you have to say about this issue. Daren, you first, please share what you think and how you feel."

"I guess to put it in perspective, I believe that Chris has become a very strong and influential person. He has a special calling upon his life and has received supernatural favor. I am not sure if he should lead us, but I have to say it would be a good idea to give him a chance. He can show us if he is ready."

"OK, and how about you Jessie?"

"To be honest, Zaga, I love and respect you so much. You have done great things for me, and took me in when I was a cast out. You will always have a place in my heart for all of that, but I feel the same way as Daren. I believe Chris needs to show us that he is ready and can do it."

"Thank you so much, Jessie, for that kindness and respect. So, Thomas, I won't even ask you because I think you feel the same way as the others."

"Well, gee, Zaga, thanks for speaking for me, but YEAH! I do."

"Well, I guess there is no need to vote on

anything now is there? Chris, I will resign my position, I give you leadership and control of this group. Do as you feel lead to do and be wise for you are responsible for people and their lives Chris, be wise. I am going to make sure that we announce this to everyone, after that I will be leaving the house, I will be moving on with my life, and do what I need to do for myself. I have done enough and now it is your turn to do this."

"Zaga, thank you for this peaceful transition. I hope the best for you in whatever you do. It has been my desire to lead this group, and I feel I came here to do just that."

As the announcement went out to the group, many were shaken by it including Tanner. She cried for the better part of a week.

But as the weeks went by, she was able to cope and except things the way they are.

The time has finally come for the concert. Jessie is very excited and cannot wait to go. Chris finished getting ready and knocked on Jessie's door.

"Are you ready, Jessie?"

"Yes, coming. Well, how do I look?"

"WOW! You look great Jessie, I mean really great. I am so excited to spend this night with you."

"Me too. I am ready to rock."

As they drove to the concert, Jessie shared some information with Chris.

"Chris?"

"Yeah, Jessie!"

"I wanted to talk to you about something."

"Sure, what's up?"

"I want you to know that I am glad you asked me to come with you. We kind of shared that we each had feelings for each other and I want you to know that I want to be you're girlfriend. I feel really close to you and I have a desire to be with you."

"Wow, Jessie, that's so weird because I was going to ask you to be my girlfriend at the concert. That is why I invited you. I really like you a lot. So it is settled then, we are together. Jessie, you are my girl."

"Sweet, I am so glad. Now let's enjoy this concert."

After the concert, Chris and Jessie drove back to the house and kissed each other goodnight. The next morning, Tanner asked Jessie how the concert was.

"It was a great band. There was a mosh pit, and people were pumped up."

"That's cool, Jessie."

"Yeah, and the best part, Tanner, is that Chris and I are dating."

"WHAT? ARE YOU SERIOUS! RIGHT NOW?"

"Yes, and why are you yelling at me?"

"He is the leader of our group. Don't you think it is wrong for you to be with him?"

"No, and actually I thought you would be happy for me."

"HAPPY, Jessie, how the heck could I be happy about that?"

"I don't know, Tanner, I mean, wow, you

are acting so jealous right now."

"I AM NOT JEALOUS! Especially of you, holy cow are you that full of yourself?"

"I was just saying, because you are being a real pain about this."

"Well, sorry, I am just sharing how I feel."

"Fine, but we will keep this between us. Unless Chris tells anyone, I need to keep it a secret."

"So will I, Jessie, it is your business not mine, it is your life do whatever you want."

"I think I am already doing that."

Jessie and Tanner go their separate ways feeling frustrated and confused. This is just the beginning of the struggles they will go through with each other. Their relationship was very strong, but will begin to weaken.

Chris, Daren, and Thomas have been discussing the group. Chris tells them that they need to come up with a name for their group, because he wants to give meaning to the group. Daren wasn't sure what they would call themselves. He did not see them like a gang. Thomas suggested calling them, *The Devoted*. Chris laughed at that name and Thomas asked him why it was funny. Chris just smiled and said "Thomas, that name sounds so crazy, I understand the meaning of being devoted, but to call a group that it just sounds silly."

"Well, then fine, I guess I will not suggest anymore. What will we call ourselves Mr. Leader?"

"Hey, there is no need for that attitude, Thomas, you better remember who you are talking to. I will not take that, so consider this your first and only warning."

"Warning? What will you do if I don't listen to you Chris?"

"Let's just say, Thomas, that you really don't want to find out, so watch your step."

"Fine, Chris, whatever, you are in charge."

"I think we should call ourselves, *The Breed*."

"*The Breed*," said Daren not fully understanding the name.

"Yeah, *The Breed*," insisted Chris.

"What the heck are we, *The Breed*, of exactly?" their conversation continues.

"We are, *The Breed*, of Satan, a breed that will change the way people look at us."

"Uh, and how is that Chris?"

"We will be an inferior force for Satan, our lord, to combat the forces of false doctrine and teachings. I want to let Christians know that they are not better than us, just because we do not serve their God. We serve a greater power and I have been called to be a son of Satan and you are all under my command under the order of my master."

"What the heck, Chris, are you serious?" exclaimed Thomas.

"Yes, Thomas, I am very serious, and you better be on board since you chose to be here."

"I don't have a problem with what you're doing. I just wonder what exactly we are supposed to be doing as, *The Breed*?"

"We will discuss that at a later time, Thomas. Just go and make the announcement that we are now known as, *The Breed*."

Thomas walks through the halls of the house trying to summon everyone to gather together.

"Attention, I need everyone to come to the common area for an important announcement. This is mandatory everyone is expected to be there."

As everyone made their way to the common room, Chris begins by saying, "Thomas has an announcement to make concerning the group."

Thomas stands up in front of the group.

"We have decided on a group name. We are now known as, *The Breed*. When asked who you belong to, you will say I belong to, *The Breed*, if asked what it means just say it is my family. OK, that is all, everyone can return to their activities and we will see you at dinner."

Thomas walks over to Chris.

"Well, Chris, how was that?"

"That was just fine, Thomas, I am very happy with you."

Chris senses a hesitation in Thomas, but is unchanged in his desire to lead the group. He ignores his behavior, because he believes in the power and authority he has received.

Jessie is happy with the way things are now, with her and Chris being together, her desire for him is strong. Chris has a desire for her as well, but his main focus is to get to know his god more and more. *The Breed*, is Chris's creation, his family. He has full reign and control. Listening to the voices inside to guide him, he is in a state of mind that is going to lead down a path that is very dangerous. But this was his desire, this was his calling and he is filled with what he thinks is ultimate greatness.

There are those, who, in their hearts do not want to follow Chris into this place, but they don't have a choice… or do they? Tanner is one who is very strong-willed and is not afraid. She backs down to show support until she feels the right time to move. From what she has seen and knows about Chris, her best move will be when she can run away where he will never find her. She knows if he does, there will be great wrath. Maybe she will reach out to someone for help, and maybe she won't. The battle in her mind is about life or death. Her choice is not yet certain, and no one is aware of her real feelings or her intentions.

Chris called Daren to his office to discuss the opportunity of going out into the community to find runaway kids and homeless adults. The purpose is to find new members and recruit them into *The Breed*. Chris wants to expand the amount of people and set up channels for which he will build up an army to come against Christianity. Daren told Chris that he does not have a problem doing this, but he was concerned about bringing in people they do not know.

"You let me worry about that, Daren."

"OK, Boss, I trust your decisions."

"Good, then find an area to search in.

Show them what we have to offer and if they seem interested I will interview them. Then we will narrow down whom we will invite in. Can you send Tanner in, please?"

"Sure thing." Daren walks to Tanner's room.

"Tanner, Chris would like to see you."

"OK, where is he?"

"He is in his office."

"OK, I am on way."

Tanner stops what she was doing and walks to Chris's office.

"Hello, Chris."

"Hello, Tanner, thank you for coming. I am curious to know if I could use you for a particular mission."

"Mission?'

"Yes, a mission. I would like for you to get to know some teens in the area, find out who the Christians are, who stands against Christianity, and who don't believe n anything. You can act anyway you wish. Is this something you can do for me?"

"I think I can pull that off for you. I just have one question."

"OK, what is your question?"

"What if I get close to people who are Christians, and they want to ask me a lot of questions or invite me to their house, what do I do?"

"Well, if that happens, simply say you are on your own living here and have roommates. If asked to spend time with their family, absolutely do so. I want to get information on everyone I can. Do you accept this

assignment?"

"Yes, Chris, I will do this."

THE POWER OF GOD

"Lord, I thank you for my family. You have blessed us in so many ways and I am grateful to you. I praise your name for being our God and King. Jesus, please lift up our spirits, and show us what you would have us to do. I ask this in Jesus' name, AMEN."

"Connor, you need to hurry, you will be late for work."

"I am on my way down, Dear."

"Is everything OK?"

"Yes, Theresa, everything is fine, I just had to pray. We are starting a new project on the other side of town today."

"Oh really, what is the firm doing?"

"We are designing the new arena, but don't spread the word about it. We just won the bid and it is huge for our firm. I am not sure if I will be home by dinner, but I promise I will call to let you know."

"All right, Honey, have a great and safe day."

"Same to you, Babe, I love you."

Theresa goes back into the house to check on Stephen, because he was not feeling well this morning.

"Hey, Stephen, how are you feeling today?"

"I am feeling better, Mom, I think maybe I was just dehydrated or something."

"Well, I am going to keep you home from school today anyway, just to be sure."

"OK."

"I will go and make you some soup."

Theresa walks downstairs into the kitchen and sees Marcy.

"Oh, hello, Marcy, I thought you left for school already."

"Nope, I am taking today off, I have a lot of things that I have to get done, and don't have time to sit in class today. How is Stephen feeling?"

"Stephen is fine. He is probably just dehydrated. I am keeping him from school today just to make sure. Are you sure you should miss class?"

"Yes, Mom, I am doing fine, so missing a day won't kill me, I just have a lot of things I need to get done."

"OK, well I hope your day goes well, and be safe."

"I will, you too."

Marcy gets into her car and drives off. She is on her way to church to talk to Pastor Shane. When Marcy pulled into the church parking lot, she parked as close as she could to the office entrance. She locked her car, and made her way into the church. Once inside she told the secretary she had an appointment with the Pastor.

"All right," his secretary replied, "let me tell him you are here, please have a seat." A few minutes pass.

"Marcy, Pastor will see you now."

"Great, thank you." Marcy walks to Pastor Shane's office.

"Well, hello, Marcy!"

"Hello, Pastor Shane!"

"It is so good to see you."

"Thank you Pastor. I am here because I wanted to talk to you about a letter that was left at our house by an unknown person."

"What do you mean, Marcy?"

"Well, when we came home from church

last Sunday there was a note on our front door."

"What did the note say?"

"It said that our family might be in danger."

"In danger?"

"Yes, and I think it was left by someone who knows my brother Chris."

"I see, I am quite surprised that it is you bringing this to me and not your parents."

"Well, Pastor, my mom is busy with the kids and my dad is busy with work right now. He is getting more work at his firm, so he has been very busy but he does take the weekends off for us."

"OK, well that is good then, I am glad God is prospering his company. So back to the letter then."

"OK, well the letter was very disturbing to me, I mean for someone to say we might be in danger, does that mean my brother would actually cause harm to his own family?"

"Well, Marcy we should not assume he would do that. However I will tell you, I had an encounter with Chris, and to be honest, it really wasn't him."

"What do you mean, Pastor?"

"What I mean is I felt a strong evil presence. I think it is really controlling him. It would not be Chris hurting people but the evil within him causing the damage.

"So let me ask you this then Pastor, do you think he is demon possessed?"

"Yes, Marcy, I do. I believe he is under the complete control of the enemy and it is the enemy's goal to hurt the church and the people of God. We have protection under the blood of Jesus so the only thing that can be done is emotional pain. God will not allow the enemy to hurt us physically."

"Then maybe the danger would be more of scare tactics that would affect us emotionally?"

"Yes, that is what I think, Marcy. We need to continue to seek God and allow him to intercede on our behalf. We can use the name of Jesus to fight, but God is the one who will defeat the enemy not us."

"Well, Pastor, I really wish I knew who left the letter at our door. I know it has to be a girl because it showed a lot of care about our family. It does not seem like something a man would do."

"Well, of course, we cannot say for sure, Marcy, but it very well could be. You should pray about this, seek God, and ask him to reveal this mystery to you. Maybe He could lead this person to you in a supernatural way. This person may fear for their life, but has shown concern for the safety of your family at the risk of being exposed."

"I never thought of it like that Pastor, you are right this person may be risking their own life to keep my family informed and safe."

"This is a great possibility, Marcy."

"Well, I guess we will have to wait and see what will happen Pastor."

"That is all we can do and thank you for coming by and talking with me about this."

"As always Pastor, it is a pleasure to speak

with you. See you on Sunday."

As Marcy left the Pastor's office, she was walking down the hallway and bumped into Pastor Mark.

"Oops, she laughs frantically, "I am sorry Pastor Mark, I should really watch where I am going."

"It's all good, Marcy" as he laughs with her, "what a way to run into each other right?"

"Yeah, I guess so." "How are you doing, Marcy?

"I am well, and how about you?"

"I am doing just fine, how is your brother feeling?"

"He is feeling better, he was most likely just dehydrated."

"Oh, well, I am glad he is feeling better

then, I cannot wait to see him back in youth group."

"Yes, he will enjoy being back."

"Great, we look forward to seeing him."

"Well, Pastor Mark, I really need to be going, I have a pretty busy day ahead of me."

"All right, Marcy, well you have a blessed day and we will see you at church on Sunday then."

"Ok, Pastor, see you later."

Marcy walks out to the parking lot and then gets into her car to head back home. While she is driving and listening to music she starts praying. "Lord, please reveal to me who this mysterious person is. They have showed care to my family. I really believe, Lord, that this person needs help, and I pray that you lead them into your light."

Marcy took a longer path home so she can search for answers from God. She finally arrives back home after driving around for a couple of hours. Once she pulls up Theresa comes outside.

"Marcy, where have you been?"

"I have been out doing things, Mom. I told you I had things to do, please do not treat me like a child."

"I am sorry if you see it that way, Marcy, but I need to know these things, OK, I have lost one child already."

"Mom, seriously you did not lose Chris, quit feeling so guilty. Chris made his own decisions, you did not decide for him. He is not lost. He is just mislead right now. I do not want to hear you say he is lost and not a part of this family, Mom, he is our family and he will come back someday. That is what faith is all about hoping for things to happen. Don't forget the Word of God is still planted inside of him."

"Well, Marcy, I do not want to have this discussion right now."

"Well, you are the one who brought it up, think about the good that will come, Mother, and remember you still have a family here."

"I have things to do, Marcy, just let me be."

"Fine, but don't come down on me. I am an adult, and I do not disrespect this home."

Marcy, feeling frustrated goes upstairs to do her schoolwork. Theresa feeling sad and lonely decides to call Conner.

"Hello."

"Hi, Dear, I was just wondering what time you think you will be home?"

"It may be late, Babe, we are just finishing off some details so maybe a couple of hours."

"Wow, Connor, that is like 9 p.m."

"I know, Theresa, but this job is important. Is everything going well at home?"

"Yes, Honey, Marcy and I had a spat but everything is fine."

"Do you want to talk about it tonight?"

"No, I just want to let it go."

"That is fine, I will see you in a couple of hours."

"Ok, Connor, I love you."

"I love you too."

As the time goes by, Connor is finally on

his way home, as he pulls into the driveway he is greeted to a big hug from Theresa as soon as he steps out of the car.

"Oh, Honey, I love you so much,"

"I love you to, Babe, are you sure your, OK?"

"Yes, I am just grateful for you and our family. I know I haven't been showing it lately, but I do care about us, even Christopher."

"Wow, Theresa, I haven't heard you say his whole name in a while."

"Well, I am turning over a new leaf, and I am going to look at things as God looks at them.

The next morning, as the family was getting ready for their day, Marcy and her mother spoke briefly and hugged. Theresa realizes how important the family really is to her.

"Since it is Wednesday, and we have church tonight, I think we should be home by dinner so that we can go to church together."

"Ok, Honey, I will do my best."

"I will make it, Mom. My last class gets out at 3:45 p.m."

"All right, see you guys tonight."

As the family leaves to go about their business for the day, Theresa begins to clean the house and puts on her favorite radio station. She hears her favorite song come on the radio and she begins to sing. All of a sudden, she feels the presence of the Lord around her.

"Lord, I feel you. I feel your love all around me. Fill me with your spirit, you are my

God and I praise you. Thank you for giving your son Jesus so that I might have salvation. I pray for your guidance in my life. I want to be a Godly mother, wife, and friend. Lord, I pray for my son Christopher, I place him into your hands. Speak to his heart and let him know you are still there. Lord, whoever put this note on our door; I lift them up to you. I pray that they will heed to your voice and be embraced in all of your love. I ask these things in Jesus' mighty name, AMEN."

Theresa's spirit has been lifted. She takes Sammy by the hand, and they dance around and around. Sammy has not had so much fun with her mother for quite some time. Theresa looks at the clock and realizes time has flown by so she orders pizza for dinner.

Stephen and Marcy are the first to get home.

"Hi, Mom, we are home."

"Hey, guys, I ordered pizza for dinner, I want us to have plenty of time to be ready to go to church tonight."

"Yes, pizza!" Stephen shouts.

"I hope it is vegetarian, Mom, you know I am watching my weight"

"Don't worry, Marcy, I ordered a small just for you."

Theresa turns her attention to Sammy.

"So, Sammy, what do you think you will be doing in church tonight?"

"My teacher said we are learning about Jonah and the Whale."

"Oh, that is such a great story, you will

enjoy it so much."

"I know, Mommy, I am excited."

Conner steps through the door from work. He is the last to arrive home and Sammy is excited to see him.

"Daddy!"

"Yes, Sammy."

"I love you, Daddy, you are the best daddy."

"I love you to, Sammy."

After Conner gives Sammy a hug, he puts his things down and walks in the kitchen where Marcy and Stephen are eating.

"Hey, Marcy, what is the college group learning about?"

"Well, Dad, we are just going over some things about relationships. How to maintain the ones we have, start ones we don't have, and keep our faith and morals in place to make righteous decisions."

"What about you, Stephen?"

"We are actually going to be in adult service tonight dad."

"You are?"

"Yeah, Pastor Mark wants us to be a part of the service since Pastor Shane is teaching on the power of God."

"Oh, I see, well this will be a very good night then. We will learn and share in the message together. We better go upstairs and get ready for church"

Conner and the kids finish eating and go upstairs to get ready. Theresa is helping Sammy get ready. Once they are done, they go downstairs and wait for the others. Theresa grows impatient and yells upstairs.

"Hey, is everyone ready for church?"

"Almost we will be down in a minute." Conner yells back.

"Ok, but you need to hurry we want to make it on time."

"Ok, we are ready now meet you at the car."

Everyone jumps in the car and heads to church. On the way there, Sammy sings her favorite songs and asks the family to join in. The Smith family is now singing together enjoying the ride to church. Stephen looks out his window as they approach the church parking lot.

"Wow, Dad, the parking lot is already

getting packed"

"Yeah, it is going to be full tonight."

"Oh, boy, just imagine inside, it will be hard to get a good seat."

"We will be fine, Stephen, it is all good."

The family finds a parking spot and makes their way into the church. Stephen runs into the sanctuary to find the family good seats. The family finds Stephen and sits down just in time for church to start.

"Hello and good evening, thank you for coming to the service tonight. We encourage you to take part in worship. Here is our worship director Dan Taylor."

"Hello, Church, are you ready to sing praise to our Father?"

"YEAH!" the church screams.

"All right, here we go."

The worship team begins sing. Spirits are high and people are praising God. Once the worship concludes Pastor Shane comes to the podium.

"What a powerful praise and worship wasn't it church?" Cheers ring out all around the sanctuary. "Lets us pray, Our Father, we come before you and ask that your word speak to us. Be planted in our hearts and protect the word. Let us be receptive and ready to understand your will. In Jesus' name, AMEN."

"Congregation, tonight's message has been one that a lot of you have been waiting to hear. Let me tell you this is not a game. Again this is not a game, God does not play games but takes everything seriously. God is not to be mocked,

God is not a referee nor does He break any rules. He made the rules church, He, and He alone is in charge. He does not need us telling Him what to do. God is all knowing and all-powerful. Please hear me when I say God does not play with us. We are in a serious spiritual battle, one that has a real enemy and his name is Satan, and he is the prince of darkness.

But let me tell you, Church, the power of God is a force that cannot be broken, AMEN. It cannot be shaken, it cannot be matched, and some may challenge it but, Church, God will win every time. The same power that Jesus had on this earth, the same power God has in the eternal heavens, is the same power inside of us. He did not give us authority in His name to hide Church, but we are to fight the fight against darkness and cast out those demons using the only name that has the power to get them out and that name is JESUS."

"When you are in battle people of God, your general is the bright and morning star, the Lamb of God, the lion of the tribe of Judah. Stand firm, Church. If you encounter a demonically possessed person that challenges you, get ready for a fight. This is not a fight you will lose, Church, and let me tell you why. He that was dead is now alive and has the power. He holds the keys of death, hell and the grave. Jesus is in charge and when you speak to that demon you tell him to shut-up in Jesus' name."

"You see, Church, when you are in a battle with someone possessed, you are in charge, not because of who you are but because who is in you. So when speaking with a demon all you have to do is say, "Demon, I am not asking you but I am telling you, in the name of JESUS be gone you have no authority or power here. The power of God is here, and you must leave. Be gone right now in JESUS' name."

"Church, when that thing squeals and cries, do not be distracted. Rejoice for the POWER OF GOD has made that demon leave when it wasn't ready to go, AMEN. Lead that delivered person to Jesus and tell them they have the favor of God in their lives. Behold the Lamb of God who takes away the sins of the world, Glory to God. The power of God goes beyond deliverance from evil, it also delivers from addictions and changes lives."

We are here to praise God and to let His light shine through us, to witness His love and help change lives. Do not make the mistake of thinking you are higher than others. We are all in this together, and we will reach those God sends our way. We will not turn anyone away. It does not matter what they look like or where they come from. We will have the heart of God in this church and we will be His light in this dark hour. Let us pray."

THE RECRUITS

Tanner has accepted an assignment given to her by Chris. This assignment is to recruit people into, *The Breed*. What she will be doing is looking for teenage runaways and people who feel rejected by their families. This is a very daunting challenge, because Tanner does not feel she is where she belongs. She has felt alone since Chris assumed leadership and named their group, *The Breed*. She is confused by the name, and she definitely does not want to belong to Chris.

Tanner is worried about what is going to happen, especially now that Chris wants to bring more people into the group. Why, *The Breed*, she asks herself time and time again. She does not comprehend this and she is unsure of Chris's intentions with the new people. Tanner only took this assignment, because she is hoping she will find a way out. She is a confused 18 year old girl, and she does not talk to people about her feelings, because she is afraid of Chris.

Jessie wants to know what Chris's intentions are about, *The Breed*, so she walks to his office to discuss how things are going. Out of the corner of Chris's eye he sees Jessie coming towards him.

"Hey, Jessie, how are you?"

"I'm great, Chris, thanks for asking. I was just wondering how things were going and to find out what decisions you have made."

"Well to be honest with you, it is none of your business what I am doing."

"Gee, Chris, I am your girlfriend, how can you talk to me like that?"

"It's simple, Jessie, what I want you to know I will tell you, do not question me or attempt to think you can understand me."

"I am sorry, Chris, I did not mean to upset

you, I just thought…"

"That was your first mistake, Jessie, don't think you can understand me."

"Fine, Chris, I wasn't trying to make you so angry. Goodbye!"

"*Wow, what is his problem today?*" Jessie says to herself. "*He is being a major jerk.*"

Confused about the interaction with Chris, Jessie goes to her room to think. She cannot believe the way he acted and her feelings have been hurt. She lays on her bed and cries, until she falls asleep.

Daren went out to the streets to see what kind of potentials he could find to bring to Chris. While he is walking down the street, he sees a girl dressed in rags. He decides to approach her and strikes up a conversation with her. She tells him her name is Chelsea.

"Chelsea, do you have a lot of friends out here?"

"Nah not really, I just get by day-by-day, ya know."

"I see have you ever considered joining a group so you could have support?"

"I ain't no gang girl, Bro, I am not into selling myself neitha."

"Whoa, hold on, Girl, I am not talking about it like that, OK?"

"What you mean?"

"I mean joining a group of people like yourself where you are not judged or condemned for being who you are."

"So, what's this group all about?"

"We look after each other and we don't let people rule our lives. We have a leader named Chris who is very passionate about helping people to succeed with their goals."

"So this, Chris, guy he is in charge of you guys?"

"Well, yeah, but not to the point of telling us what we can wear or how to act. He guides us into spiritual freedoms, and he teaches us how to stand against our enemies."

"Well, that sounds pretty cool, but why me?"

"Well, you seem to not have any friends as you say and it is not good to be alone. I would like for you to meet Chris, and let him tell you more, OK?"

"Yeah, cool. I can do dat."

"Great, here is the address, you can meet me at tomorrow, and I will take you to him."

Daren continued on with his recruitment efforts, but the day seemed to drag on. Not too many people he spoke with were interested in what he had to offer. He managed to talk to a few people about meeting with Chris. The others shrugged him off and didn't care about what he had to say. At one point, one guy told him to step off or get bruised up. When Daren called it a day, he returned to the house and told Chris how his efforts went. "So, Chris, things didn't go so well for me today."

"What do you mean?"

"Well, I talked to a lot of people, and man I will tell you there are a lot of people that are sore in their hearts. People didn't want to hear me and told me to leave or get beat up. I was able to reach a girl named Chelsea and a few others."

"What did Chelsea have to say?"

"Well, she is alone here and seemed interested as soon as I told her about us. I told her to meet me at the secondary address, and then I would bring her to you for an interview."

"Ah sweet, sounds good, does she seem vulnerable enough to join us? We need more girls here. I will sweet talk her into joining if I like her."

"Yeah, it seems like she would join us. So then what should I do? Just focus on girls or what?"

"No, talk to everyone you can. If you find

people that is receptive, put on your charm and invite them to talk to me."

"OK, Chris, sounds good, man. I will head back out tomorrow."

When Daren leaves Chris' office, Chris gets up to go into the hallway. He wants to talk to Jessie about their argument.

"Jessie," Chris calls, "hello, Jessie, where are you?"

"I am upstairs, what do you want?"

"I would like to talk, can you meet me down here in the common room, please?"

"Fine, I will be there in a few minutes."

"OK, I will be waiting."

As Jessie prepares to go downstairs, she wonders what he would want to talk about.

"OK, Chris, what do you want?"

"I wanted to apologize for snapping at you today. I should not have done that. I want you to know I will work on treating you better."

"Good, because you really hurt me you know, I thought we were a team since we are together."

"Well, we are together, Jessie, but we cannot be a team the way you see it. I am in charge and responsible for everyone here and for bringing in more people."

"OK, now that you brought that up I have a question. Why do we need more people?"

"We need them because that is what I was told to do. We need a greater force than just the small group we are. We need to be a force to be seen and recognized. I am building a following, and I want people to see that we are just as real as their Churches are."

"Well I can understand that and thank you for answering my question."

"You are welcome, Jessie, but for future reference, just try to see what I see and don't question me in front of any members got it?"

"Yeah, Chris, I got it, I will not do it again."

Tanner has now returned to the house from being out trying to recruit people, but she was not so lucky in her search. She did not find anyone she felt comfortable bringing in. As she goes upstairs, she hears Jessie crying and decides to knock on her door.

"Hello, Jessie?"

"Yes, who is it?" Jessie responds with a

sniffle.

"It's me, Tanner, is it OK if I come in?"

"Yes."

"Are you OK, Jessie?"

"Yeah, I am fine, I just have some issues with Chris. I do not like the way he is treating me. One minute he is nice and considerate, and then the next he is rude and a jerk. He only cares about himself."

"Ah, so relationship issues, I mean, it will happen, you guys will not always get along, you know."

"I know, Tanner, but he won't listen to how I feel."

Tanner begins to laugh.

"Well gee, Jessie, that is like almost every guy out there."

Jessie starts laughing too.

"Yeah, I guess you're right. Oh man, it feels so great to laugh."

"Yeah, well you know what they say, right?"

"What's that, Tanner?"

"Laughter is medicine to the soul, and girl we need to laugh with all we got going on."

"Yeah you are not kidding. Sometimes I feel so stressed out like things are so one sided and we can not do anything right."

"I know what you mean, Jessie, it is like Chris changes so much day to day. How in the world can you predict him, you know?"

"I know, Tanner, trust me I know, but I really like him and I will never leave him. I want to be the only girl he wants, so I will never leave *The Breed* or him."

"Well that is your choice, Jessie, but not all of us feel the same way. I am not sure if this is what I want the rest of my life to be like. I would like to live and meet a nice man and have a family someday."

"That is great, Tanner, but you know you are not going anywhere unless Chris decides he is either done with you or you just disappear. And I am not suggesting that you disappear either, because he will find you."

"I am not planning on it, Jessie. I just want the chance at a real life, and that is why I came here when Zaga offered to take me in. I wanted to get on my feet, but I don't even have a job or anything. There is nowhere to go, I am here and that is that. I know Chris has great intentions, but he must know we have our own lives."

"Well, let's talk about this some other time OK, I don't think it is wise to talk right now."

"OK, I will catch up with you later."

"OK, Tanner, see you later."

As Tanner walks out of Jessie's room and makes her way down the hall, she runs into Thomas.

"Hi, Thomas, how are you?"

"I don't know, Tanner, why don't you tell me."

"I don't understand, what do you mean?"

"I overheard you and Jessie talking, OK, I know you are not happy here."

"That conversation was between us, as friends, just sharing some feelings to vent,

Thomas, and you had no right to listen in on our conversation."

Tanner tries to walk away.

"Where do you think you are going, Tanner?"

Thomas grabs her arm.

"Get your hands off me, Thomas! I mean it, let me go."

"Fine, but just remember I know what I heard, and I cannot promise that it won't get back to Chris."

"Do what you want, you jerk, I don't care. I will tell him you got physical with me, and he will not like that."

"Whatever, Tanner, you little rat, you are no one special here. He could care less if someone hurts you."

"Whatever, Punk!"

"Watch yourself, Girl, that's all I am saying."

Tanner feels cornered and sees no way out. As she yells Thomas leaves.

"Chris," Tanner yells, "Chris, please where are you?"

"What, Tanner, what is wrong?"

"Thomas was listening to a conversation between me and Jessie, and we were just venting some feelings, and when he saw me in the hallway, he grabbed my arm really tight."

"So he restrained you from leaving?"

"Yes, Chris, that is exactly what he did."

"Thomas," Chris yells, "Thomas, come here right now."

"What, Chris, what's the big uproar?"

"Tanner said you violated her and Jessie's privacy, and that you restrained her from leaving, is this true?"

"Well first off, I did not violate anything, I was walking by and heard her say that she was not sure she wants to be here."

"That's not true, Chris, he is a liar! I never said that!"

"What did you say then, Tanner?"

"I said I wanted to have a life where I could be married and have a family that is all."

"OK, understandable, but you know we are your family and you have that freedom here, you will live with us and we will be together, right?"

"Yes, Chris, I know that. But why did he have to treat me that way?"

"Thomas, you will apologize to her right now."

"Fine, Tanner, sorry for grabbing your arm."

"And Thomas, if you touch another female here, I promise you will regret it, understand me?"

"Yes, I understand you."

"Good then."

Now that the big scene is over, Tanner goes to her room upset and cries. She hopes she will not be under watch because of what happened.

Chris makes his way to Jessie's room. He wants to get her side of the story. He knocks and she opens the door.

"Hi, Babe."

"I am not here for romantic talk, Jessie."

"Uh, OK, what is going on?"

"I want to know about the talk you and Tanner had, and don't dare lie to me because I know that you two talked."

"Well, she heard me crying because I was upset about how you were treating me."

"OK, and what did she talk to you about?"

"She said that she wanted to have the type of life where she could have a family."

"Is that all?"

"Well no, she also said she didn't know if she would be here her whole life."

"So she intends to leave us?"

"Well maybe, but not us as in you and me, but the group."

"I don't care how it is meant, Jessie, we are

all a family here. She needs to understand that we are here for each other. This is not a prison where you have fear. We are offering freedom to be whoever you are. I don't need any trouble. We are *The Breed*, a group of people open to serving one god and that god is Satan. We are a special breed. We rule with his will and we accept new people based on the same principle. He is in charge, Jessie, and he uses me to guide us where we need to go. Tanner needs to embrace what we are and how we work."

"And if she decides not to, Chris?"

"Then she will regret knowing us."

"That is not freedom, Chris. You are saying she cannot leave if she wanted to."

"NO THAT IS NOT SO, if she leaves, she

must be punished for leaving her blood, her god and her leader, period."

"That is insane, Chris. She has to have permission from you or our god, as you put it, for her to live the life she wants to live?"

"EXACTLY, JESSIE, THAT'S THE WAY IT IS, PERIOD!"

"OK, fine, Chris, just don't yell at me like that!"

Jessie heads down to Tanner's room to let her know what is going on.

"Hey, Tanner, hello, are you in there?"

"Who is it?"

"It's me, Jessie."

"Yeah come in, Jessie."

"Hey, I just wanted you to tell you Chris knows how you feel."

"So what, who cares anymore."

"You should because he will not let you go, Tanner, you have to ask permission to leave and you know that will never happen, so you must come to terms with, *The Breed*."

"I will do as he wishes, OK, I will not cause any issues. You can tell him that I will do whatever he needs me to do. I will hit the streets again to find recruits to join us in his mission. I will try to bring in more females."

"What do you mean more females, Tanner?"

"That's what he told me, he wants me to bring more girls into, *The Breed*."

"Well he must have a reason for that, so I guess just do your best." "I will do my best to please him. I am going to go to bed now I am really tired, OK?"

"OK, Tanner, you get some rest. You need it."

Jessie leaves Tanners room. Tanner is left feeling lonely. She is worried about what could happen to her if she tries to run away. Will Chris go after her? Will he hurt her if he finds her? She is unsure and wonders if she has the courage to find out.

Chris is not happy about the situation with Tanner. He is not sure if she will try to leave. He has no intention of letting her go so he makes his way to Daren's room.

"Hey, Daren."

"Yeah, Chris, what's up?"

"Hey, I need a favor from you."

"OK, what's up?"

"I need you to find someone to keep an eye on Tanner."

"Why?"

"I just need to know where she is and who she is talking to since she is supposed to be recruiting for me. I need to know she is doing her job."

"OK, no problem I will take care of it."

"Good because I need to make sure she does not pull any stunts."

As Chris gets up to leave he sees Thomas pass Daren's room. Chris jumps up and runs to the door.

"Thomas, please come with me."

"Hey, what's up, Boss?"

"Thank you for going along with the whole apology thing."

"HUH, what do you mean?" "I mean I don't really care if you apologize or not. Tanner needs to be kept in check, but do not put your hands on any girl in this group, OK?"

"OK, Chris, no problem."

"I need to have you do some shopping?"

"I do not want to go out alone right now."

"Take another member, and get what's on the list, nothing more and nothing less. We have some preparations to make so make it quick?"

"Ok, be back soon."

The next morning, Daren's recruits show up at the address they were given. Daren and Tanner met the recruits and drive them to a local abandoned storage shed. As Tanner and

Daren lead them across the tracks, to the building, the people seem a little scared.

"OK, people, here we are, when you see Chris you will show your upmost respect and hear what he has to say. You will answer only when spoken to, and that is it. Chelsea, you go first with Tanner and good luck."

"It's OK, Chelsea, let's go."

As the two enter the building, they come to the center and stop.

"Hello, Chris," says Tanner with Chelsea at her side.

"Hello, Tanner and who is this we have here?"

"This is Chelsea, and she would like to see if she is worthy to be a member of, *The Breed*."

"Chelsea is it?"

"Yes, Sir."

"My name is Chris, I am not a sir. Please feel free to call me Chris, OK?"

"OK, Chris, it is an honor to meet you."

"So tell me, Chelsea, why do you want to be in, *The Breed*?"

"I was told you take people in without judgment."

"This is true, Chelsea. We are family here, would you like to be a part of this family?"

"Yes, Chris, I would."

"Are you aware we serve someone?"

"I know you serve the devil, and I don't care I just want to belong somewhere."

"Well, Chelsea, today you have been truly blessed because you are a perfect fit for our family. Welcome home, Sister, welcome home."

"Thank you so much, I am so thankful."

"Tanner, take our new sister home, please, and show her to her room, and introduce her to the family."

"Yes, Chris, right away. Let's go, Chelsea, come on."

As Chris interviews the other recruits, Tanner gets Chelsea back to the house and does as Chris instructed. Everyone was friendly and took to her very well. The other recruits were also accepted, except for one, Scott. Chris felt he was not a faithful man and would not be of interest to *The Breed*. Therefore, he was dismissed. In all reality, Chris felt he could have been a spy sent to see what was going on in the house. He wasn't taking any chances with him.

The others, Bruce, Jeremy, Claudia and Raymond, are in the age range from 16 to 20 years old. *The Breed* is getting bigger, and the mission is getting underway. The recruits will serve a great purpose, and Chris cannot wait to see how far into the darkness they will go. He is teaching hatred with the deception of love and once unleashed the community will see something they have never seen before. What will happen next is under lock and key.

GOD'S PLAN

"WOW, Connor, what an amazing church
service that was tonight, I mean the pastor
really went out and finished strong. I felt so
convicted during service because I feel like we
are staying in our comfort zone. We really

should be out ministering in our spare time to reach the lost for Jesus. God is really moving in me, Honey, I feel a passion to reach out to someone. I don't know what it is or who I am supposed to reach but I just have a fire burning inside."

"That is amazing, Babe. I know that whatever God has for you, He will lead and carry you through it. I hope we can help those in need. You are right we need to step out of our comfort zone and do more. It really seems that God has given Pastor Shane a strong message and he is letting it be heard."

"Hey, Dad." Marcy calls.

"Yeah, Marcy, what?"

"I don't think Pastor Shane really wants a message to simply be heard. I believe he wants the message to take a new direction with actions and not just words. Actions speak louder than words, Dad, and I think that is what he is trying to say here. We are to come out of our comfort zone like Mom said, and actually penetrate the areas where the devil has a stronghold."

"That is a very good point, Marcy, I think you have heard what you needed to hear. We really need to see where to go with this. I don't know what God has in store with this at all. Maybe we are to do this as a church body, reaching out to our community or maybe it is for us on individual levels. I don't know yet."

"Connor," says Theresa, "it could be both you know, God could be calling us to reach out in both ways. All I know is there is a real spiritual battle going on and many people don't even know they are in it. What do we do when we run into someone who is possessed?"

"I know what we do," said Marcy, "we beat that spirit up with the power of Jesus name, and we stand firm in His presence, and allow the power of God to remove that spirit and then once the person is delivered we talk with them about Jesus. Tell them they have been delivered and that they need to accept Jesus as their Lord and Savior."

The family continues their talk about Pastor Shane's message all the way home. Once they got home, they all went about their business. Connor, who has been working on a huge architectural project downtown, is still drawing up some plans for his next presentation. This is something that can really launch his firm, and give him some significant recognition. His project has been in the works now for about six months, and he is working hard to land this contract.

Marcy is working hard with her studies, and of course, her college social life. She is more focused on her schoolwork, instead of going out with friends at church. She has a secret crush on a certain someone, but has not told anyone about it. She is not sure if it is the right time, but she wants to tell him. Maybe she will write him a letter and explain her feelings.

Stephen is working hard on his music and guitar playing. He is really doing well and enjoys playing in the youth group band. The youth will be attending a youth conference in a few months. The youth pastor told him his band would be playing a song during the worship service at the conference. He is really excited, so he is practicing a lot.

Theresa and Sammy have been reading in the children's Bible so Sammy can learn more about God. Sammy, who will be turning six years old soon, loves reading her Bible and praying with her mom each and every night. She often tells her mom she is praying for her big brother Chris. Even though she barely knows Chris, she has a strong devoted love for him. Sammy tells all of her friends at kindergarten that she loves Jesus and that He will help them with everything. She has such a young, sweet spirit.

The next day, everyone met for breakfast

and then went on their way. Once Stephen got on the school bus, some friends asked him about his brother. Stephen told them he does not know where his brother is, and he has not spoken to him. Chris has been gone for a long time and Stephen is not interested in answering questions about him.

On the way to college, Marcy noticed some people talking on a street corner. It seemed odd to her she thought they were doing something suspicious. While stuck at the light she prayed and asked God if she should pull over and talk to them. She called her mom and asked her what she should do. Theresa told her to keep going and not stop, because it was not safe to stop alone. Marcy kept going but felt guilty inside for leaving.

Once at school she could not concentrate in any class so she decided to skip her last class and go see Pastor Shane. When she got to the church she walked in and asked the secretary if Pastor Shane was available.

"Yes, Marcy, he is. Let me tell him you are here."

"Thank you," Marcy replied.

"Ok, Marcy, the Pastor will see you now"

"Great, thanks again."

Marcy walks into Pastor Shane's office"

"Hello, Marcy, what a great surprise to see you."

"Oh yes, Pastor, I am sorry to just drop by, but I really needed to talk to somebody."

"Tell me, what's on your mind?"

"Well, Pastor, since your sermon last night

I have been confused about what to do. I drove
to school this morning and saw some people
talking on a street corner, and well I thought
maybe I should stop and talk to them about
God."

"And did you?"

"No, I did not. I called my mom, and she
said just keep going that it was too dangerous to
do it on my own."

"I can see her point, Marcy, she is a parent
concerned about her child. Even though you
are an adult, you will always be her child."

"I know, Pastor, and I respect that so I kept
going. I just felt so guilty for leaving, and I
have been down ever since. I even skipped my
last class because I could not concentrate all
day.

"What can I do to help you, Marcy?"

"I just need answers, Pastor. I need to know what to do when I come across opportunities when I am alone."

"Well, Marcy, all I can say is listen to your heart. You will know when God is leading you somewhere, and when He is telling you to stay away. I know you have a real desire to get out and reach people and that is great; however, you need to yield to the Holy Spirit and let Him guide you."

"How do I discern, Pastor? How do I know when God is leading me to do these things?"

"Marcy, that is something you will feel inside, when God leads you I believe you do not have to second guess because He is there with you. He will never leave you when He is leading you to do His work. He is always with you. You see, Marcy, when God calls us to fulfill a plan He has called us to, He will never leave it unfinished. I believe we have a calling to see people delivered from demonic possession. There is such a dark cloud over parts of our city, and we need to fight the powers of darkness. We can no longer just go to church on Sunday and Bible Study on Wednesday. We have to get out there were the battle is and take back that which the devil has stolen. Your own brother has been taken away by lies and deceit. He has been blindfolded by the enemy and sees things that are not real. He does not think with a clear and free mind. He is a prisoner in his own body because the enemy has taken him captive. I know it is hard to hear, Marcy, because he is your brother and you love him, believe me I wish I could go run and bring him home to your family today. But there are many people in our city that are affected by this. They do not see what is really happening and follow the lies thinking they are truths. All we can do is obey God's plan with the guidance of the Holy Spirit. God has His plan for each of us but we are all a part of His biggest plan, Marcy. That plan is the salvation of the lost and to deliver those in captivity."

"That is a great way to put it, Pastor, I need to find something inside myself to hear Him. I think I have been so closed off to what He wants me to do, because all I can think about is finding my brother and getting him back. God will do it in His time as you say but until then I need to see what His plan is for me."

"That is right, Marcy, focus on now, and what God will have you do. He will lead you to the bigger plan that He has when you are ready."

"Thank you so much, Pastor Shane, I really appreciate your council as always."

"Well, Marcy, you are very welcome, that is what I am here for. Now you make sure you focus on your schoolwork too!"

"OK, Pastor I will."

As Marcy leaves Pastor Shane's office, she could not help but stop by Pastor Mark's office. Marcy knocks on the door.

"Hello, Marcy, how are you?"

"Oh, I am OK. I hope I am not disturbing

you."

"No, not all, how can I help you?"

"Well, I just wanted to tell you that Stephen has been so excited about the youth conference coming up and he is practicing a lot. I know he must be nervous, but he is just so excited."

"That is great, I am glad he is working hard."

"Yeah! Well, I wanting to talk to you because, I am, uh.."

"Marcy, are you ok?"

"Yes, I really am okay. I just, well, I wanted to tell you I have been trying to get through some things that have been making my life crazy."

"Like what? Can you give me an

example?"

"Well, yeah of course. So you see, I have had a crush on you for some time now."

"OH, I see. Well, that is interesting."

"Why is that interesting, Pastor Mark?

"Marcy, I have had a crush on you too."

"Really?"

"Yes, and since I am a Pastor, it seemed a little out of the sorts to approach you. I mean we are very close in age, and you are a very smart girl. I will just have to say there is nothing we can do about this until I take care of something first."

"What would that be if you don't mind me asking?"

"I would like to talk to your mother and father and Pastor Shane about this. I would like their permission to move forward with any relationship."

"I can respect that, Pastor, and do it when you feel it is the right time."

"Will do, Marcy, you have a great day and tell Stephen I said he is doing a great job."

"I sure will, and you have a blessed day as well."

Marcy got in her car and started heading home she had such a glow about her. She was listening to her music and singing loudly. She is so excited about Pastor Mark liking her. As she turns the corner and is about to come to a red light she stopped the car. Once the light turned green, she hit the gas and headed through the intersection, when out of nowhere, a drunk driver ran the red light and t-boned the passenger side of the car. The truck hit her with such force that it pushed her clear into the other side of the intersection. The airbags deployed, and glass shattered everywhere. Smoke came from the tires as they screeched, before the vehicles finally came to a stop.

A man walking his dog witnessed the whole thing and immediately called 9-1-1 to tell them about the accident. Emergency responders came very quickly and they immediately checked on the passengers. The driver of the truck was unconscious. The emergency responders are going to have to get him out fast and rush him to the hospital, because he was bleeding from his eyes and nose. When they went to check on Marcy, they did not see anything physically wrong with her.

"Ma'am," they called, "can you hear me? Hello. Can you answer me? Are you in any pain?"

There was no reply from Marcy.

"Captain, there is no response."

"Can you get her out?"

"I think so, but I am not sure we should move her. I don't know what injuries she has since she cannot answer me."

"Get her out on the board strap her down and put a brace on her neck. Check her ID so when we get to the hospital we can call her parents."

"Yes, Sir, come on guys, let's get her out of here as gently as possible. OK, on my count, one, two, three lift. Let's secure her, and get her out of here."

As the emergency responders get the passengers ready for transport to the hospital, the police start asking witnesses about what happened. The man, walking his dog, told them everything he saw. Others could only give a little bit of information. Police would have to pursue the video from the traffic light to see exactly what happened. Marcy and the truck driver are put into the ambulances and rushed to the hospital, but remain unconscious. Once at the hospital, they are taken into separate rooms to be evaluated.

"Doctor?"

"Yes, nurse what is it?"

"We have a young woman we have identified as Marcy Smith. Should we call her family?"

"Yes, immediately please, now let's get her in here for examination. Marcy can you hear me? HELLO, MARCY, RESPOND! Let's get her hooked up and keep an eye on her vitals.

The drunk, truck driver has finally come to. The doctor is working on him and thinks he may have a brain injury. The driver has been identified as Travis Keller. As the hospital gets ready to call Marcy's family, the police arrive to report the findings on the accident.

"Have you contacted her family yet Nurse?"

"No, we are just about to do that."

One of the policemen standing in the room speaks up.

"Please allow us to do this as we were on

scene.

"We need to contact the truck driver's family; as well his name is Travis Keller."

"Ok, we will take care of it."

The police arrive at the Smith home and knock on the door. Theresa answers the door.

"Hello, is everything okay, Officer?

"Ma'am your daughter, Marcy, has been in a very bad accident and is down at the hospital right now."

"OH MY GOD, NO!"

"Ma'am, please come with us, and call who you must; we need to go right now."

"Yes, of course," Theresa crying really hard is trying to pull it together so she can go.

As the police take her to the hospital, she calls Connor and tells him what has happened.

He instantly rushes from work to the hospital. Once there, he calls Pastor Shane and tells him what happened to Marcy. Pastor Shane leaves the church in a hurry and heads to the hospital.

Once everyone arrives, they are asked to be seated in the waiting room until the doctor has a moment to update them on Marcy's condition. Connor, Theresa and Pastor Shane all huddle and begin to pray for her as they weep in sorrow.

Lord, God, we are here humbly before you and ask for your hand upon Marcy. Lord, please guide the doctors and give them the knowledge to help her. Father, we ask in Jesus' name for her recovery, Lord, we also ask for the other driver in this accident, Lord, be with him and his family in Jesus' name, AMEN.

"All we can do now is just wait and hope all is going to be fine," said Pastor Shane.

"I can't lose another child, Pastor, she has to be fine."

As Connor and Theresa hold each other crying, all they can do is hope for the best. The family of the other driver has now arrived at the hospital. The two families stay separated from each other so there is no interaction. Time is passing slowly, and Connor remembers someone needs to pick up Stephen and Sammy. He looks at Theresa.

"Someone needs to get Sammy and Stephen."

"Don't worry I will have someone pick them up and bring them here," says Pastor Shane.

Eventually the children arrive at the hospital. Sammy is crying while Theresa holds her and Stephen is crying in his father's arms. Finally the doctor comes in and asks to speak with Marcy's parents.

"Mr. and Mrs. Smith, I am Dr. Noel. First and foremost she is alive. Second we did a CT scan and it shows Marcy has bleeding in her brain. This is certainly causing her to remain unconscious at this time. We need to have a surgeon come in and relieve the pressure and then we will cross our fingers for the best."

"Of course, doctor," says Connor, "please do what you have to do to save my daughter's life."

The doctors rush Marcy into surgery to begin relieving the pressure off her brain. The family waits patiently in the waiting room with Pastor Shane. All they can do is pray and wait. Connor calls his parents and tells them what has happened and to pray for Marcy.

"Of course we will pray for her Son, Tell her that we love her and are praying for her and a full recovery."

It has been hours and still no news about the surgery. Pastor Mark has arrived to get an update on her condition. Pastor Shane tells him the diagnosis and that she is in surgery.

"Pastor Mark thank you for coming," says Stephen, "it means a lot to have you here."

The doctor comes out and meets with the family and their Pastor's in the waiting room.

"Mr. and Mrs. Smith, Marcy is doing well, she has made it out of surgery successfully."

"Oh, that is great news, Doctor."

"Yes, but please keep in mind we are not out of the woods yet. She still has to recover, and once she wakes up she may not remember things. She could have memory loss, short term or long term, we just don't know enough right now. The best thing you can do for her now is pray."

"Can we see her please?" Theresa asked.

"Yes, of course, but only a couple at a time."

"OK, Doctor, thank you."

Connor and Theresa go into the room and see Marcy hooked up to machines and her head bandaged. They cannot help but cry. They take her hands and kiss her on her forehead as they tell her they love her. They leave the room crying holding hands. Stephen goes in with Pastor Mark. When Stephen sees Marcy, he starts crying. He walks up to her and yells for her to wake up. He turns around and runs into Pastor Mark's arms. They cry together for a little while.

Stephen and Pastor Mark come out of the room and reunite with the rest of the family. Theresa is having a hard time dealing with this and turns to Pastor Shane.

"Pastor Shane, is this God's plan for Marcy, for our family? We lost Chris already, what will happen if we lose Marcy too?"

"God's plan is one we all seek and are called to, Theresa. We must have faith in God and be strong for Marcy. I know this is hard. You have to believe and lean on God's strength.

He has a plan for us all and He will show us this in His time. Please go home and get some sleep you will need your rest. She will want you here when she wakes up, I am sure of it."

"No, Connor. I can't leave my daughter here alone," says Theresa, "I will sleep here and be with her. You can take the kids home, but I am staying with Marcy."

"OK, Babe, I understand, just try and get some sleep."

"OK, Honey, be safe, and I will see you in the morning."

"Thank you Pastor Shane and Pastor Mark for coming," Conner and Theresa say simultaneously.

"Of course, please keep us updated on her progress," Pastor Shane replies back.

Everyone but Theresa leave the hospital. When Connor makes it home with the kids, he puts them to bed. As he lies down in his bed, he begins to pray,

"God, I am not sure what parts of life are in your plan, but, Father, please take care of my daughter. You are our God. You sit on the throne and rule over all the Earth. May your will be done in Jesus' name, AMEN."

DISSERTED

It has been two months since the new

recruits have been accepted into, *The Breed*,

and Chris has intensified his plans. Chris's

hunger for a larger group has been growing and

his efforts have been paying off. Jessie has

been talking to as many girls as she can to recruit them. She has been telling them they will be housed, fed, and they will have all the support they will need.

Jessie and Tanner have been at odds with each other since the last incident. Tanner has been keeping her distance, and Jessie is doing her part, by spying on Tanner and keeping Chris up dated. This is the one thing that Tanner absolutely hates. She knows she does not have privacy or freedom, even though Chris does not give her the impression of being spied on and he insists he is fine with her. Tanner is beginning to crave freedom. She wants so much to live a free life.

Chris is about to call a meeting to give

important information to the group.

"Hey, Daren?"

"Yeah, Chris."

"I need you to call everyone together for a meeting in twenty minutes."

"OK, Boss."

Daren walks through the house informing every one of the meeting Chris just called.

"Everyone, listen up we are having a meeting in 20 minutes. Chris said everyone must be there, no exceptions."

Jessie hears the announcement and yells to Tanner.

"Tanner."

"Yes, Jessie."

"You know we are having a meeting, right?"

"Yes, Jessie, I am aware of it and I will be there."

"OK, will you make sure Chelsea knows, because she was not present for the roll call Daren gave?"

"Yes, I will make sure she knows."

Jessie walks to Chelsea's room.

"Come on, Chelsea," says Tanner, "we better get going downstairs for this meeting."

"I am coming, Tanner"

Tanner and Chelsea walk to the main area where the meeting will be held. Chris is standing up front of the common room waiting for everyone to come in and be seated. He tells Daren to make sure everyone is there and then make an announcement about him delivering a message.

"OK, Everyone," says Daren "come on, Everybody, let's go already, we need to get started." He turns to Jessie for help. "Jessie, pass around the roster and make sure everyone signs in please."

"Yep you got it."

"OK, Everyone, let me have your attention please, Chris has things he needs to speak to us about, so give him your full attention. These issues are important and you need to listen. Chris is a great leader, and he wants only the very best for us. It is time to begin so everyone here is Chris."

"Thank you, Daren and, hello, Breed members."

"Hello." they all replied.

"I am so thankful for all of you. I am

pleased to be your leader and to act on everyone's behalf. We are entering a new phase, a new chapter if you will. I am going to be assigning units within our breed. I want us to have sections where each of you will be a part of a specific mission. It is important that each of you have a full purpose and a full understanding of that purpose. You will swear an oath to, *The Breed*, and me. I will require all of you to do this whether you are new or have been here a long time.

This is what you will say, 'I, state your name, do hereby swear my life service to, *The Breed*. I swear to uphold the orders and fulfill the mission even if it takes my life. I will fight against Christians, those who hate me for who I am. I will not have mercy on them for they have none for me. I will stay true to my fellow members and not betray them, if I do, I will be punished by death.' This is what you will swear to, this is to honor our cause and to honor each other. Do not betray your brothers and sisters.

Do not be like the blasphemers. We are set apart. We are higher and called to a better purpose than those heathens. Are there any questions?"

"I have a question." A member replies.

"State your name." says Chris.

"My name is Bruce, and I am a relatively new member, I was just wondering about the whole death thing. How would you get away with killing someone if they betray a brother or sister of, *The Breed*?"

"Good question, Bruce, and I am pleased to

answer. You see it is like this; most of you are runaways, outcasts or have no one, no family. This is your new family, and we are your brothers and sisters. If you betray us and are put to death. Tell me, Bruce, who will miss you, look for you, or report you missing? You could be dumped into a ditch and found. No one would even care who you are. Just another homeless person who dies and no one cares that you are gone."

"Anyone else with any questions? No, good, then let's move on. You were chosen to be here, and you are not free to leave. We will serve our master and as his chosen, you will do as I say and you will serve our mission."

Now that Chris told them what is expected, he has everyone raise their right hands and swear the oath. How deep is Chris willing to go? How much further will he travel before things get more dangerous? He is now telling people to lay down their lives to save him. He has come to a level of selfishness that insures his survival, but not the survival of the other members.

"Now," Chris says, "everyone will understand why we are here. I am going to divide, *The Breed*, into sections. Daren you will be in charge of section one and your mission is to get the lay of the land. I want to know how many churches are within our radius and then how the immediate area feels about Christianity. I want to know what types of churches are here and the average age of its congregation. You will achieve this by attending the churches.

Jessie, you will be in charge of group two. You will be responsible for getting support from the locals who are homeless, runaways, and people who are angry at society. You will explain to them what we do. You must send out your forces and talk to these people. Get them on our side without membership so they can be our eyes on the street. We will pay them for their efforts with food. If any of them lie to us or betray our trust then you know what you must do.

Group three, will be headed up by Thomas. Thomas your group's responsibility is to study where pastors live. When Daren reports his findings to us, I will then ask you to track down these so-called "Men of God." I want this information so when the time comes we can attack. We will show these people that we are the majority with the power of our god and we will destroy them, their mission, and burn their buildings.

Finally, group four, will be headed up by Tanner. Tanner will be responsible for enticing young men to get close to their families. I want to know who and where these families are, what they do, what their schedules are and most importantly, the right time to move on them once trust is established. I want to steal their kids, turn them to our side. If the parents get in the way with their preaching, then you convince the kids that their parents are liars. Do whatever you have to do to accomplish this.

I want a rebellion of epic proportion to take

place. I want to make these kids think we like them and have them fight with us. Now to all of the sections you need to listen to me. One area you will not go into is Maple Street on the Upper East Side of town. That area is off limits and if you go there you are done. I will find out and I will finish you personally do I make myself clear?"

"Yes," they all answered.

"Good, then we understand each other."

Jessie approaches Chris once the meeting is over to ask him about the Upper East Side.

"Chris."

"Yes, Jessie."

"What is the big deal with the Upper East Side and Maple Street?"

"Don't worry about that, Jessie, when the

time is right that is my part of town and I will take care of my own. That is the last chapter of my life I will finish."

"Ok, that is a good enough answer for me."

Now that all has been said and sections have been assigned, everyone is preparing to go out into the city. Some are still unsure of what is really happening. Perhaps they don't have a full understanding of what it would be like joining, *The Breed*. They knew they wanted something different and thought joining the group would be good, because they fit in. But now things are different. It seems like they are supposed to worship Chris. This seems to be a little off to most members, but they do not dare to say anything about it.

Tanner, who has always felt that Chris is trying to gain power and control of everyone, is right. She is so upset about what Chris just announced. She cannot believe she had to swear an oath to him and, *The Breed*. This is something Zaga would never do. He would never approve of this, because he cared about the people he took in. Tanner misses Zaga very much. Now that he is gone, she does not know what to do, but go along with Chris's plans.

Daren has already started make plans for his section. He will have most of his people go out in small groups to see what types of churches are in the area. They will need to get the service information, what kind of people attend, and their age. He will then sort out the options of churches to be targeted. Once his group attends the churches and gathers all the relevant information, Daren will report his findings to Chris.

Jessie is extremely excited about her section's mission. She is very hopeful that her group will do the task exactly as Chris wants it. She wants them to excel beyond all expectation, because she has a desire to please Chris. She started by having her group talk to youth runaways in order to entice them into the group.

Thomas is at a stand-still until Daren gets the information back to Chris. Once it is done, Thomas will work with his group and find out where these pastors live and get as much information on them as possible. Thomas sees himself being able to get some dirt on them like a politician would do to his opponent. Tanner is not speaking to anyone and is very unsure about sharing her feelings with anyone. Little does she know, but she is under constant watch. Chris has assigned a member to keep a close eye on her, to make sure she does what she is supposed to do. Chris has little regard for her feelings and just wants her service. Jessie however has a special place in Chris' life and no one is allowed to mess with her.

Chris decides to go into his room and spend some time alone, since the sections are busy with their missions. His room is dark and dreary. He has pentagrams and goat heads on the walls and floor. He has a small desk where he studies. There are small, dull candles illuminating enough light to see. Chris closes his eyes and begins meditating. This is how he puts himself into a trance and contacts the spirit world. He is disciplined and patient, he waits until he hears from the spirits.

All of a sudden, evil fills the air. Chris feels a slight breeze on his skin. He clears his mind and hears a moan, he knows, they are here.

"I am here, lord. I am your servant, here to please you and do your will."

All of a sudden, he is lifted off the floor in a seated position. Chris feels the presence and power of the devil. Chris feels so honored to be picked by Satan that a single teardrop falls from his left eye. At last an evil voice speaks to him.

"It is your lord and master, Satan, and I am well pleased with you."

"You are my god, I bless your name and worship your majesty".

"My son, you are all I could have hope for. I will empower you to be my light to shine into the world polluted by false truth as God has done. I was cast out for speaking my heart, as were so many others in my world. I will use you to show them what my love and freedom really is. That people can be free to choose what they want and not be punished for their hearts."

"Should I call you Lucifer or Satan?"

"Call me Satan, for Lucifer was cast down from heaven and now Satan rules the world for truth. Together we will gain a presence here to combat God and His so-called followers, to me they are robots following orders based on a book."

"Yes, this is what I want. I want to show them they are nothing."

Time seemed to stand still as Chris and Satan talked. Chris has been suspended in mid-air the entire time, he is being held and moved by the powers of darkness. Chris does not like to be disturbed during this time, but there is a knock on the door. He does not answer. The knocking continues, but he does not hear it.

After knocking several times, Tanner decides to open the door. She knows not to bother Chris while he is in meditation, but she cannot understand why he is not opening the door. She opens the door, and sees Chris floating in the air. She is startled and frightened, but cannot escape. As she stands in the doorway and evil voice squeals and rushes the door. The spirit throws Tanner out of the room, and the door slams shut.

Tanner, now in tears, runs to her room and closes her door. She is sitting on the floor with her knees in her chest, crying, because she has never seen anything like it. Fear has multiplied and she feels threatened. What will she do now? She has entered into the room knowing she should not have. Chris will be very angry and she fears his wrath. She does not dare to tell anyone, because she has no one to trust. What will she do? She ponders in her mind. *"What will happen to me now? I have invaded his privacy and I saw him standing in the air. That is not right. It is not normal. He truly has the power of the devil and I am scared. What is really going on here*?"

Tanner is traumatized by the whole experience. She knows she has to make a decision, fast. She cannot stay in the house. Now is the time to go. She gathers her things together and sneaks out of the window. She has disserted, *The Breed*, and her life is now in danger.

END OF BOOK ONE

ABOUT THE AUTHOR

James W. Owens Jr. was born in Orlando, FL in 1976. He grew up in Deltona, FL and has lived in Colorado and Texas. James now resides in Pennsylvania. He has served in the United States Army, and is a disabled veteran. He is married and has two step-children.

15440838R00116

Made in the USA
Charleston, SC
03 November 2012